ELISABET VELASQUEZ

WHEN WE MAKE IT

DIAL BOOKS

DIAL BOOKS

An imprint of Penguin Random House LLC, New York

First published in the United States of America by Dial Books for Young Readers,
an imprint of Penguin Random House LLC, 2021

Copyright © 2021 by Elisabet Velasquez

Dial & colophon are registered trademarks of Penguin Random House LLC.
Visit us online at penguinrandomhouse.com.

Library of Congress Cataloging-in-Publication Data is available.
Printed in the United States of America
ISBN 9780593324486
1 3 5 7 9 10 8 6 4 2
CJKV
Design by Jason Henry | Text set in Chapparal

Poetry is the way we help give name to the nameless so it can be thought.
—Audre Lorde
Poetry Is Not a Luxury

Dear Reader,

When We Make It is based on my life growing up in Bushwick, Brooklyn, at the height of the "war on drugs" and as gentrification accelerated. Like Sarai, I am a first-generation U.S. born Puerto Rican. My family also navigated mental illness, houselessness, and food insecurity, and lived significantly below the poverty line. Making it was often both as simple and as complicated as hoping the pantry box included a really good name-brand cereal, or having heat in the dead of winter.

I wrote this book as a way to acknowledge these truths and to honor those who've experienced the same. Some of the poems in *When We Make It* touch upon sexual assault, abuse, mental illness, miscarriage and pregnancy. And so, there may be poems that hit close to home, poems where you might want to pause and take a break after reading in order to process. Please take the time you need.

I also hope there will be poems that make you laugh and that fill you with wonder and hope.

I am only here because I remembered who I was. I was born already forgotten. This book is for those born with stories already erased. May we return to them in whatever way rings true. This book is also for anyone who feels their emotions before they can name them. For anyone who still may not have all of the language but has their story. Your story is all the language you need. And of course, this is only one story of many. I urge you to write *yours*. All of our stories are pivotal & necessary on our way to making it.

Thank you for reading,

Elisabet Velasquez

FALL 1996
BUSHWICK, BROOKLYN

"QUE CANTE MI GENTE"

—"MI GENTE"
HÉCTOR LAVOE

HOW I GOT MY NAME
SARAI

Let's start the story where abandon meets faith.
Aight, so, boom. Check it.

I'm named after a homegirl
in the Bible who couldn't have kids.

Her man Abram was all like:
Yo, Sarai, God promised me I would be the Father of Nations.

Sarai was all like:
Nah B, you must be buggin', you know I can't have no babies.

Our pastor says faith is believing in something
you can't really see.

According to Mami,
we should never put our faith in men.

Mami was pregnant with me when Papi bounced
for some new chick & told Mami to have an abortion.

Abram got himself a new chick, too.
Got her pregnant and all that.

I guess Mami identified with Sarai's fear and doubt—
& so I was born out of Mami's faith & hope.

MAMI

Mami is a round woman.
A square by any other definition.

No-nonsense, Pentecostal
with no patience for her own children most days.

There are three of us in total.
Danny, Estrella & Me. I am the youngest.

My sister Estrella said Mami's depressed.
File this under "shit we don't talk about."

Pentecostals, we're just supposed to pray
the sadness away.

¡Fuera! The pastor demands on prayer night.
¡Fuera! I imagine sadness is a bad singer

being kicked off the show
by el Chacal on Sábado Gigante.

Apparently, Jesus & Don Francisco
can save anything.

Once during church testimonio,
Mami gave Jesus mad credit

for saving her from Papi's fists. *¡Amén! ¡Aleluya!*
Now, Papi lives in the Bronx with his new wife.

Estrella uses the payphone
to collect call him all the time.

She says Papi is also Christian now
& that God forgave him

for beating on Mami & so we should too.
But Mami's eyes never close right during prayer service

& I wonder what kind of God you have to be
to receive praise from the hands responsible for that.

HOW WE GOT OUR NAMES
ESTRELLA

Estrella was named after another woman
Papi was cheating on Mami with.

Nobody says that out loud though. But I can tell
by the way my sister's name jumps off of Mami's tongue

like one of those side chicks
on *The Ricki Lake Show*.

On my father's tongue, Estrella matters.
Her name is a sloooow dance in Brooklyn.

Her name is a bullet that didn't kill nobody.
Her name is the beeper alert that gets a call back.

Estrella is three years older than me.
She is sixteen but her body is not.

She got that *it's not my fault,*
I thought you were older kind of body.

She is the kind of beautiful
that dique puts men in danger

or that makes men want to be dangerous.
The kind of beautiful Mami always wanted to be.

When we walk down Knickerbocker Ave.,
the men hiss like they are deflating at the sight of us.

They call Mami suegra. Mami can't stand it.
Qué ridículo, she says.

She ain't old enough to be nobody's mother-in-law.

She shifts her body in front of Estrella's,
to protect her

or maybe so she can be seen first.

PAPI

Estrella races to the window
and pulls back the curtain,

which is really just a fuzzy blanket
with a lion print that Mami ordered from Fingerhut,

a magazine that lets Mami own nice things
and pay for them slowly.

Papi parks outside and makes his station wagon cry
until it guilts Mami into letting us go downstairs.

I examine my father until he is human again.
When he hugs me, I want no parts of his hands.

I become Mami the last time he hit her.
Leave me alone. Don't touch me.

Estrella laughs at my fear & tells Papi
Mami is brainwashing me into hating him.

Papi says he hopes
I'm not becoming an angry bitch like Mami.

Men don't like angry bitches.
Men leave angry bitches.

All Mami was ever good for was kicking him out.
He can't remember the last time

her mouth made a home for him.
That's why he left

and didn't come around for a few years.
Now Papi comes by every weekend

& gives us five dollars to split.
Estrella & me argue over how to spend it.

Five dollars
can buy us mad chips,

quarter juices,
Now and Laters, Devil Dogs.

Or we can use it to share one ham & cheese hero
and a two-liter.

When I look up at the window
you can't see Mami peeking but

the lion's mouth is open
and roaring for me to come upstairs.

LUCKY

In Bushwick, the reporters double park
to shoot the latest crime scene & then bounce

quick before their news vans get tagged up.
The teachers find their car radios missing

and blame the worst student they have.
Pero, the teachers and the reporters, they get to leave.

Back to their "good" neighborhoods
with boring-ass walls and vehicles

they don't have to piece back together like a puzzle.
They'll have a nice dinner with their predictable family

and talk about their wack-ass day in Bushwick
& somebody will say: *You're lucky you don't live there.*

Someone else will echo: *Imagine?!*
& they think they can imagine because fear

got them believing they know what it means to be safe.
I mean, it's one thing to feel danger.

& maybe it's another thing
to work in it.

& maybe it's another thing altogether
to live with it.

But it's something else completely
to be the thing everyone is afraid of.

WE AIN'T AFRAID

Estrella says:
We ain't afraid of nothing.
We ain't afraid of nothing.
We ain't afraid of nothing.

I say:
Some days though,
shit is scary.
Not gonna front
like shit ain't scary.

Estrella says:
Damn, yo, what's so scary?
That's just Corner Boy Jesus and his friends.

I say:
Shit. That's 5-0. Ayo!
They're creeping around the corner.
I tell Estrella & the corner boys to run. Run!

Estrella & the corner boys say:
Run? We ain't running.
Snitch? We ain't snitching.

Estrella says:

Yo, chill, we'll be aight.
Yo, chill, we'll be okay.
& even when we not
we are. You know what I mean?

& I know exactly what she means
'cause it's just like being afraid.
Even when we not we are.
Even when we not we are.

      But I don't say that.

      Nah.

I don't say that.

NEIGHBORS

Bushwick is full of hip-hop & salsa.

Cuchifritos & soul food.

Nail & hair salons.

Bootleg CD vendors & tamale ladies on the corner.

We are all the same in our difference.

No matter how we got to be neighbors here

We all know we lived somewhere else first.

I know this because on the occasion that

Our eyes lock for more than a moment

Our mouths ask each other the same question.

Where you from? Like nice to meet you.

Where you from? Like what block?

Where you from? Like what country?

Where you from? Like what God?

Where you from? Like where you been?

Where you from? Like where you going?

Where you from? Like who you missing?

Where you from? Like why you here?

Where you from? Like have you gone back?

Where you from? Like what did you leave behind?

CURIOSITY KILLED THE CAT SATISFACTION BROUGHT IT BACK

Mami says ¡que soy *entrometida!*
& she's right,

I'm always asking
about things I shouldn't be.

Estrella thinks I ask a lot of questions 'cause I'm dumb.
Being a dumbass has its rewards though. She laughs.

She means that in Bushwick,
there are some things you just don't wanna know.

That way you sound believable if the cops ever ask you
something where the answer could get you locked up or killed.

But I know asking questions
is sometimes the smartest thing I could do.

It gives me permission to not know everything.
Besides, answers are just questions

that haven't been discovered yet.

I ASK QUESTIONS ABOUT PUERTO RICO

When I ask Mami to tell me about Puerto Rico
she says it's none of my business

and that I should focus on school.
How is where I am from none of my business?

I decide to talk back today.
You are not from Puerto Rico.

You are Nuyorican,
Mami says.

A Puerto Rican born in New York.
Does that make me less Puerto Rican? I wanna know.

Sí. No. ¡Qué sé yo!

Mami is annoyed
& tells me to stop asking questions & pack my clothes.

We are moving.
Again.

LEAVING GATES AVENUE

Mami never has money for the bus or cabs
so we walk our belongings to the new spot

on Knickerbocker Avenue.
We gotta stop at the Check Cashing

to get a money order for the week's rent.
I'ma miss writing Gates Avenue on the money order.

It always felt super appropriate considering that
everything in Bushwick looks like it could hurt you

if you crossed it.
All the buildings are built like weapons.

Even our schools are gated &
the welfare office is spiked

as if to let you know
that you are entering a war zone.

We order Chinese food through glass
that might stop a bullet

but can't stop a kid with a blade
and a dope tag.

Windows are secured with metal bars &
roofs are fenced in with barbed wire.

In this way even the sun becomes a criminal
if it sneaks into an armored building.

At the Check Cashing spot the pen is chained
to the counter & today I stole it

just to say I set something free.

HOW WE GOT OUR NAMES
HOOKERBOCKER AVE

is what everybody calls Knickerbocker Avenue.
& since names have a way of making things true
Mami has a warning for Estrella & me
as we leave the new room
we're staying in to go buy pizza for dinner.
She tells us to come straight home
& not to stand on the ave. for too long.
 Si te coge la jara no hay dinero pá sacarte.
Which is to say you can't even trust the cops
to tell the difference.
Which is to say Puerto Rican girls
always look like they're for sale.
& for a brief second I wonder what I'm worth.
What it would cost to keep me for a night.
What it would cost to set me free.

TODAY IN BIBLE STUDY
TRINITY

We learn:

God the father.
          God the son.
               God the Holy Spirit.

Are all the same.
Are all different.

I'm not even gonna front like I get how that shit works.
But if I had to share my identities with two other people
I'ma pick the underdog. The one who flies mad under the
radar but does some powerful ass shit.

That's the Holy Spirit in this case.
I mean, sure, Jesus turned water into wine
and did the whole *I'm dead...SIKE! I'm not dead* bit
but have you ever seen the way the Holy Spirit
possesses a body and makes it dance across the room
without hitting any of the furniture?

That's talent.

I guess what I'm saying is that I think I'm talented

enough to make it out of here
while avoiding everything
that tries to get in my way.

SARAI'S GOT TALENT

Actually, I don't really know if talent is the way
out of the hood.

There are mad talented people in Bushwick
who are still here.

Like the ladies who make the toilet paper doll covers
made of yarn

& the hood musicians who record
then hustle their mixtape on CDs on the ave.

& the street chefs who make the most bangin' empanadas
and tamales that you'll never find

in any restaurant
& the acrobats who swing their bodies

on an L train pole in the name of showtime.
& the writers who tag up the walls with their names

so colorfully that you couldn't ignore them
if you wanted to.

Mami says my talent is being nosy.
I say my talent is paying attention.

ROSTER

I know the moment right before
the homeroom teacher
is about to call my name off the roster.

A brief silence stings the air
while all the kids with heavy names
sink their bodies into the chair.

My best friend's name is Lauricia,
which people always wrongly pronounce
Larissa or Laurish-a.

So she just tells people to call her Lala
to avoid the exhaustion that comes
with correcting people.

Lala & I can tell who has a "good" name
by the way they chew their Bubble Yum
mindlessly or scratch the date on the wooden table.

Our mouths do not get the luxury of rest.
Our mouths must always be war-ready,
which means, sometimes we rip our names

from the teacher's mouth
before she has a chance to kill it,
but other times we wait.

After all,
the teacher is human, like us,
but more real.

Maybe we wait to see if this time, she will get it right
or maybe we are waiting to see if our name
can be held in a mouth that is not our mother's.

THE COOL PUERTO RICAN
ENGLISH TEACHER

Ms. Rivera looks & talks wild familiar.
Like she could be my cousin or something.

How funny it would be if
Ms. Rivera was really just a cousin I didn't know.

Ms. Rivera could even be me. Yo. Maybe she *is* me.
The me that finishes school & gets a college degree.

The me that learns how to talk proper and shit.
The me that owns a car and lives in a good neighborhood.

The me that makes mad money, or at least enough
to make sure we always got food in the fridge.

The me Mami couldn't be.
The me Estrella doesn't want to be.

The me that makes it
for everybody that couldn't.

HOW WE GOT OUR NAMES
MAMI'S JOB

When Ms. Rivera asks me what Mami does for a living
I don't know how to make her sound important

enough to mention.
You know the kids who have parents with good jobs

by the way their hands shoot up
and shake until they're chosen.

*Let's hear from someone
we haven't heard from yet.*

Ms. Rivera scans the room for those of us hiding
our hands, our eyes, our lives.

Mami sews people's clothes, I say.
A seamstress.

Ms. Rivera gives Mami's job a name
that sounds valuable. Names can do that, you know.

I shrug. All I know is that she works
in a factory making clothes

& she'll never know the people who wear them
and they'll never know the lady who made them.

OFF THE BOOKS

Mami gets paid off the books.
Off the books is another way to

say that you're sneak paying someone
to do work for you that you'd probably

have to pay them more for
if they were on the books.

This may seem unfair.
But being paid off the books means

Mami can get extra help
from the government.

At the welfare office
the caseworkers try to convince Mami

to tell them the truth by acting
like they care about her.

They tell her that working off the books
means she's being taken advantage of.

But Mami tells us that if she were on the books
she wouldn't get paid much more than she is now

but it would be just enough
to make her not qualify for food stamps.

& that makes me wonder about
who is taking advantage of who?

HOW WE GOT OUR NAMES
HOMEGIRLS

Even though Mami warns me against having friends
I love my homegirl Lala.

Lala is an only child. She lives with her mom
and her dad & they got a house

with a basement and a back yard
and Lala even has her own room.

Lala's mom is a nurse
and Lala's father works at a bank.

Good jobs.

But Lala's parents want her to do better than them.
At lunch she tells me stories about hosting sleepovers

for her cousins and for the friends whose parents
allow them to stay in casa ajena.

They order Tony's Pizza & dance like the Spice Girls.
I always crack the same corny joke

and say we would be the
Adobo Spice Girls.

I guess they call them homegirls
because friendships have a way of making you feel safe

& most people feel safest at home.
Sometimes when I see Lala in the hallway

at school she leans in close enough
for me to smell what her mom made for breakfast

and I give her the hungriest hug.

THE NEIGHBORHOOD IS CHANGING

Someone is always fighting in Bushwick.
I don't remember the last time I walked down the street
and someone wasn't angry at something.

El Señor who sells the gallon jugs of maví leans over
and inspects the wheels of his cart
while muttering curse words directly at the spokes.
It may seem silly to be so angry at the wheels, but I get it.

It's necessary for everything to work smoothly
when you're walking down a Bushwick sidewalk.
These streets are not for standing still.

That's why Mami yells at us to hurry up
as we roll our own cart filled with compra
from Scaturro, the fancy supermarket
we shop at when Mami gets paid

from her job at the factory.
Mami says: *If you're going to be a target*
you should be a moving one.

El Señor and his carrito, however,
are not really concerned
about being a target.
He's been selling maví in Bushwick for years.

Maví is how he pays his rent & he makes a killing
because you can't find maví in supermarkets.
Mami always stops and buys a jug for her

and a cup for me.
It's all the old man has, she says.
I'm not used to her being so kind.
I side-eye the drink

and wait for her to look away
to dump it in the sewer drain.
The new people on the block

who look too young and too white
to be his customers are angry too.
I wanna laugh and say:
Welcome to Bushwick

but they'll know I don't
mean it. They're so tight that
in their rush to nowhere

they've almost tripped over
the crazy old man yelling at his wheels.
He's far from crazy though.
Since they've just moved here,

I know things they don't know,
like how his anger doesn't come from the fear
of dying from standing still,

it comes from the fear
of not being able to move
enough to live.

STORYTIME WITH SEÑOR MAVÍ

Señor Maví has all the stories.
He was around back when Broadway got burnt

to the ground.

¿Tú sabías eso? he says.
Mil novecientos setenta y siete.

Señor Maví talks slow & raspy.
His voice is so hypnotizing

it can almost carry you directly
into the flashback.

The 1977 Blackout
had everybody wildin' out on Broadway!

¡Se llevaron todo!
Televisions, furniture.

Señor Maví said he even
copped himself a new mattress.

People took what they needed.
& they needed everything.

Señor Maví said in his time
people really struggled.

Not like now.
We don't know shit about struggle.

Señor Maví sounds like he's asking himself a question:
¿Los muchachos de hoy en día?

And then answers it.
No saben ni un carajo lo que es sufrir.

I wanna ask Señor Maví about his struggle.
I wanna ask him about how he got here.

But instead I ask him for permission.
Can I be Puerto Rican?

CAN I BE PUERTO RICAN?

If I was born in Brooklyn?
If I've never been to Puerto Rico?
If I mix my English with my Spanish?
If I cop quenepas from the Chino spot?
If I don't know the Boricua national anthem?
If I can't name *our* national heroes?
Can I be Puerto Rican?
If the closest I've come to the beach is la pompa?
If I can't dance salsa?
If all I got is a feeling?
Can I be Puerto Rican?
If all I got is a feeling?

IF BEING BORICUA IN BUSHWICK IS A FEELING— IT'S THE BEST KIND

It's throwing your body in front of la pompa
when the block is on fire.

It's searching la basura for an empty Goya can
to stab into a sprinkler system.

If being Boricua in Bushwick
is a feeling, it's chasing *el piragüero*

to cop a cherry icee for you &
a hielo de crema for Mami.

It's buying Trapper Keepers from the 99 cents store
on Graham, Myrtle and Knickerbocker Ave.

It's shopping on any ave. except 5th.
Unless 5th is hosting the Puerto Rican Day Parade.

Then you buy flags off Papo's carrito
& plaster everything you own in it.

It's the smell of arroz con gandules y una chuleta
bien sazonada, seasoning the hallway to el apartamento.

It's talking to God. It's talking about God.

It's the best bochinche ever.

It's música del Diablo
blasting out of Honda Civics.

It's música de Jesucristo
blasting out of Pentecostal churches.

It's buying pollo from *el vivero*
instead of *el supel-melcado*

a reminder that something
always has to die

for you to survive.

BEING BORICUA IS NOT JUST A FEELING

Señor Maví is offended that I would even say that.
Qué feeling ni feeling.

Ju Boricua or Ju No?
When he is talking English

Señor Maví's accent leaves out certain letters
& emphasizes others.

Some people will argue that he's saying it wrong
but I like to think he's making a choice

on how much English gets to live
on his tongue at a time.

What makes somebody Boricua?
I ask a question & pose a challenge.

Primero tenemos que bregar con la historia.
I think Señor Maví means that being Puerto Rican

concerns a history I don't know
& one I must learn.

HOW WE TALK
BORICUAS

We don't say listen up
We say: ¡Mira!
We don't say we're surprised
We say: ¡Chacho!
We don't say we're poor
We say: *La piña está agria.*
We don't say that sucks
We say: *Ay bendito.*
We don't say what a mess
We say: ¡Qué revolú!

Today, I overheard the bodeguero Goldo
use all of these while talking to a customer.

Mira. ¡En qué revolú me metí yo mudándome pá acá!
¡Chacho! Y estoy estoquiao, porque la piña está agria.

& all the customer could say back was:

Ay bendito.

PRONUNCIATION

We can tell who is from the neighborhood
and who isn't by the way they pronounce
street names. We pronounce Graham Avenue
not like the cracker (GRAM) but like if
the first half of the word got stuck in your mouth
and you had to breathe out to let out the second
(GRAA-HAM). Some people say we are saying
it wrong but they are just jealous our accents
want every letter to be heard because isn't that the worst
thing? To exist so plainly in sight and still be ignored.

PLANCHA

If Estrella's hair was a street name

it would be hard to pronounce.

Estrella has mad hair.

You couldn't ignore it if you wanted to.

I know because it's my job to iron it.

We don't have an ironing board in our new small room.

So Estrella sits on the floor against the bed.

I section off her waves until they lay flat

on the bed like dead lightning bolts.

I press until she is Pantene Pro-V beautiful.

If Pantene Pro-V hired models from the hood,

Estrella would have a job.

Except that the girls in the commercials

have good behavior hair

& Estrella's hair is that disrespectful

talk-back kind of hair

the kind you can hear yelling

on the other end of the telephone

the kind you hang up on.

GOOD HAIR DAYS
BAD HAIR DAYS

On the good hair days, Mami braids Estrella's hair firmly
because loose, free-flowing hair is for putas y piojos.
Today is a bad hair day. Estrella said she didn't care if
she looked like a puta or got head lice. She's wearing
her hair loose no matter what. Mami didn't even let
her finish being disrespectful before her hands dove
all into Estrella's hair the way pigeons dive towards
the concrete when the block viejitas feed them
breadcrumbs.

No matter how shiny I make Estrella's hair look, it will
always dull in Mami's hands. This morning, Mami's
grip is on point. This exact scene has happened so
many times, it's almost like they've memorized their
moves. Mami knows the perfect way to steer Estrella
across the floor like a mop & Estrella knows exactly
how to rise from the floor like steam.

GOD & LUCIFER

Estrella & my birthdays both fall on holidays.
She got Halloween & I got Nochebuena.

When Mami is buggin'
she says our birthdays are a sign

that Estrella belongs to the Devil
& I was chosen by God.

Mami barks at Estrella & has her kneel on a pile of rice.
I used to have to ignore Estrella or risk my knees too.

But then I started sitting on the rice
just so Estrella wouldn't be so alone.

Now whenever Mami tries to separate us
we lock ourselves in the bathroom & laugh

like two old friends
reuniting in heaven after so long.

ESTRELLA TURNS SEVENTEEN

She's finally the age of our favorite magazine.
TLC was on their cover this year & Estrella said

maybe one day we could be on somebody's cover all
crazy, sexy, cool.

In Bushwick, everyone is the star
of their own tragedies.

We don't call our lives a tragedy
but the newspapers do.

The newspaper got the best bochinche about us.
The newspaper is like that one kid in class

who always talking mad shit about you
when you not around

but won't ever say it to your face.

THE DAILY NEWS SAYS

The Daily News says we all carry knives.
The people who carry knives say they gotta watch their back.

The Daily News says we are all on welfare.
The people who are on welfare say nobody would hire them.

The Daily News says we all end up pregnant.
The people who end up pregnant say:

Are you gonna take care of my kids?
No? Then mind your own business!

The Daily News says we're all on drugs.
The people who are on drugs say they just wanted to escape.

The Daily News says we're all drug dealers.
The people who deal the drugs

say they're providing the escape.
Then there are the people The Daily News

doesn't report on at all.
People like Ms. Rivera, Lala

& Lala's parents.
People like Mami, Estrella & me.

The people at *The Daily News*
have a story to print.

The people in the streets
have their own story to tell.

& I'm writing my own story
so that I can remember it accurately

in case someone else
tries to tell it for me.

DEVOTIONAL

In church everyone has a role to play
if you're in good standing with God.

You can be a preacher, play instruments,
teach Sunday School, or even help people to their seats.

The pastor has given me the role of devotional lead.
This means I open up the service by singing.

This is an important role because it sets the tone.
Too many hymns and people might fall asleep

but pretend they're praying.
Too many coritos and the Holy Spirit

might take over.
Which is actually exciting

but it makes the service longer.
The man who plays the piano says

we can rehearse
if I want so he can get to know my voice.

Piano Man is so supportive.
He also offered to teach me

how to play the drums
since the church is missing a drum player.

Maybe playing the drums could be a new talent
that might even get me on the cover of *Seventeen* magazine!

The first Puerto Rican Pentecostal drummer
from Bushwick to make it there.

Anywhere.

WE'RE SORRY THE WELFARE OFFICE IS CLOSED AND WILL REOPEN WHEN YOU HAVE NO BUS FARE TO GET HERE

In another language
we have it all.
Goodness is our inheritance.

In this language
the case manager assigns an ID card to remind
us that goodness can be taken away

& we gonna need to reapply.

In this language
Mami doesn't laugh
so loud or dance so publicly

or love us too much
so much
that we forget
the scraping sound

at the bottom of the pot
the burnt taste of tomorrow.

TOY DRIVE

Since Jesus decided to be born
at the end of the month

we have to wait on line
with everybody else who's broke

by now. Mami asked
if they were giving out coats this year

but they said they didn't get enough
donations for a coat drive.

Estrella & I asked the lady
if she had Barbies, and we got them.

Some people will say we're too old
to be playing with Barbies.

But it's either that or settle
for gloves & scarves.

Since we can't watch TV,
Estrella & I use the Barbies to create

our own live action novelas.
Estrella's Barbie lives in the mansion with Ken

and rides the pink corvette.
The pink Corvette didn't come with the Barbies,

so we make one
out of an inside out cereal box

& Tropical Fantasy caps
& waste one whole pink crayon to color it.

The mansion is on our windowsill
& we pretend Barbie

has a view of a neighborhood
with streets with names

that end in Place, or Drive.
Estrella makes my Barbie the maid

and says I'm lucky to even be in the house.
I think this storyline is mad boring so I refuse to clean

the window so I can add some drama like in real novelas.
Estrella gets mad and tells my Barbie she is fired

and kisses Ken
to celebrate.

I light up a paper towel on the stove
& start a small revenge fire

on the first floor of the mansion.
If I can't have a good life too,

none of us should.
Estrella pats down the burning curtain

and saves her pretend life.
I throw my Barbie at Estrella's face.

She throws her Barbie at mine.
It's just a game, stupid, she says.

You act like this is actually real life.

BIRTHDAYS ARE THE WORST DAYS

I turn fourteen today
      but around here we only remember things

that matter.
Things that matter pay the bills.

    The teachers say all I gotta do is get good grades
        and graduate to make it.

I've always been an honor roll student
so maybe that means one day I'll be an honor roll worker.

      It's not that I'm any good at school,
it's just that I know how to follow the rules.

Estrella says rules are meant to be broken
      & my teachers say that's why

she's never gonna do nothing,
never gonna go nowhere, never gonna be somebody.

I got dreams because I have to have them.
I got dreams 'cause I wanna wake up one day

to a Happy Birthday.

WE NOT CATHOLIC

Mami doesn't want me wearing the cross
Lala gave me for Christmas

because it sports a dead Jesus on it.
Mami says Jesus is alive even though

nobody in Bushwick has ever seen him
anywhere other than on the rosaries

in the hands of the Italians,
possibly praying for us to leave the neighborhood.

Catholics keep their Jesus laid up
on a wooden cross everywhere you can think of.

Dead Jesus crosses, dead Jesus paintings,
dead Jesus candles and statues and Bibles.

Dead Jesus is a constant reminder
that love requires sacrifice even though

we never asked for him to die in the first place.
Just like how Mami

always reminds me she almost died
giving birth to me. Points to her C-section scar

that goes from her belly button to her breasts.
But I never asked to be born.

You would think Mami would appreciate the cross.
This in your face *I suffered because of you* stuff.

But no, we gotta keep Jesus in our hearts,
which is stupid wack

and my heart got way too much shit in it already.

I THINK WE MAY BE HOMELESS

but I'm not sure.
Today is our first day back from winter break.

Ms. Rivera thought it would be dope to start the year
writing good things about our home.

What makes our home special?
Is it the room we sleep in or the people we share it with?

Maybe it's a meal we eat or a tradition we follow.
I already hate this assignment

but if I wanna make Ms. Rivera–type money
I gotta be the first in my family to graduate 8th grade.

I told Ms. Rivera I didn't understand the assignment.
She looked at me like she wanted me to be someone else.
Someone who didn't ask questions. Someone who
didn't make her work so hard.

I try not to make teachers angry so I explained
that where I live changes all the time

and we eat the same thing every day.
I wanted to add *if we even eat at all*

but I figured I said enough.
That's just how it is where I'm from.

That's just how it is.
& don't we all got the same story anyway?

Ms. Rivera asked me if I was homeless.
I'm shocked. I can't believe she tried to play me

in front of the whole class.
Yo. I looked up to her!

Don't people who are homeless sleep on the street?
You tryna say I look like I sleep on the street?
Homeless Miss. Home-Less.
The word is literally self-explanatory.
Are you dumb?

These are all the things I should have said but I didn't.
So, I just laughed 'cause sometimes laughter
is the only thing that makes sense
when you're angry.

People who are homeless
don't have a home and we do. Right?

Our home is wherever we need it to be.

THINGS YOU CAN'T DO TO SURVIVE: BREAK THE RULES

We're moving again.
We usually move whenever Mami finds
a cheaper place to stay through word of mouth.

Today, I found a section
in the back of the newspaper
that advertises rooms for rent

& Mami gave me a quarter
to run to the payphone and call the ad
and act like her.

She's afraid if they hear her accent
they won't rent to her.

I can sound like a white girl on the phone
if I pronounce my r's and say the word *great* a lot.

It must have worked 'cause the Italian man
said we can stay there for three weeks.

We'll be sharing the kitchen
and the bathroom & we have to follow his rules.

There's nothing new about following
somebody else's rules.

The only new thing is
the person who's making them.

THINGS YOU MUST DO TO SURVIVE: BREAK THE RULES

I am just finishing in the bathroom
when the Italian man starts chasing me
                                  down the long hallway that
leads back to our new room.
            Homeboy is screaming like I clogged the toilet
or something.
                        He is shaking my wet panties in his hands.
    I guess I forgot to take them off the shower rod
                    when I finished washing them.
  Mami hears the escándalo and comes out of the room
                        just in time to pull me inside
and slam the door in his face.
He starts banging on the door
and calling Mami a *puttana*
                which I'm not sure
but sounds like it could be puta's Italian cousin.
He ain't never even slept with Mami
        but all it takes for you to be a ho is a man's anger.
Anyway, homie starts wrestling his keys
        against the doorknob.

But Mami always says if you want to survive in this
city you have to break the rules.

                    & changing the locks is about survival.
Mami says she never trusted no man
    to respect   her space
even when they sign a contract
    promising they will.

SACRIFICIO

Everybody makes sacrifices.

That's what Mami says when

she's trying to justify leaving

the Italian man's room

with no real place to go.

It's for our safety, she says.

But we don't really feel safe anywhere

so who cares if we get yelled at

by a grumpy old Italian man.

Mami cares.

Mami cares so much that

tonight we sleep in a church.

The hardwood benches

are not meant for tired bodies,

but tonight they are the perfect

shape for our slumped skeletons

just like a lidless casket.

Near the altar,

Jesus almost looks asleep

on his own wooden bed.

BROOKLYN WELA

I went to visit Brooklyn Wela today

'cause Mami needs twenty dollars for food.

Brooklyn Wela is Papi's mom.

She lives in a two-story house on Suydam Street.

Mami waits for me up the block on the corner

inside the chicken spot

which is where we'll get dinner from

once I cop the twenty bucks.

She doesn't want to step foot on Wela's block

and risk running into Papi.

Wela asks for Mami.

I say what Mami told me to say:

She's not feeling well.

Wela's eyes are small buttons

that fasten her wrinkles to her doubt.

¿Qué le pasa?

Wela knows English but won't speak it to save her life.

She's given enough of herself to this country

and I guess she's decided that she'll keep her tongue.

I don't know, she's just sick.

¿Qué?

She understands but wants to hear me talk in a language

that Mami should have taught us.

Está enferma.

Wela gives me a twenty and some yerba buena

for Mami's sickness.

I don't say it out loud

but I know that only one of these green things

will make Mami feel better.

THINGS WE DON'T TALK ABOUT
COLOR

When describing Wela everyone uses the word *trigueña*
which means not white but not Black either. There are
pictures of Welo hanging on the walls of Wela's
apartment. Papi looks just like him. Welo looks like
a white guy, I laugh. *Sí, tu abuelo era blanco así como tu
papá.* Brooklyn Wela explains that Welo & his parents
were born in Puerto Rico but their parents were from
Spain. Brooklyn Wela says her father was blanco too
and her mother was Negra. *¡Pá que lo sepa!* That's all
she says about that though. This was not meant to be
a history lesson. Just a fact. I don't hear anything else
about this fact. Nowhere. Not in the kitchen. Not en
la sala. Not from Papi. Not from Mami. Not when the
neighbors talk to Wela like she understands English.
That's all Brooklyn Wela will ever say about that.
We'll never get no other details. Not casually.
Not in conversation. Pá que lo sepa. Just so you know.

¿PASTELÓN O PERNIL?

Sometimes I get to chill with Lala's family
after school while Mami finds us a new place to sleep.
Lala's mom asks me what I want for dinner
in a way that makes me suspicious.

I'm not used to having options,
so I say *whatever* in case it's a trick question.
No. Not whatever.
Tell me what you want.

I want to try something new for once.
I want to know what choice feels like on my tongue.

I want to know the shape my mouth makes
when what comes out of it matters.

I want to be asked again
just to make sure I heard right.

THINGS WE DON'T TALK ABOUT
COLOR

Lala & I talk about everything.
I tell her about Wela and Welo & how cool it is that

Puerto Ricans are White & Black & Brown & Beige
& every shade and color

that we don't even have names for.
Lala said she gets called Negrita & it's mad annoying.

I know. I agree.
I'm tired of everybody calling me Blanquita

like I'm some gringa or something.
Lala says it's not the same thing.

What do you mean?
Lala repeats it like she shouldn't have to.

It's just not the same thing.
She sucks her teeth & that's all she says about that.

& just like Brooklyn Wela,
this wasn't meant to be a history lesson.

Just a fact.

WHEN SOMEONE ASKS IF YOU HUNGRY THE ANSWER IS ALWAYS NO EVEN WHEN IT'S YES

Lala's mom drops me off & tells Mami she fed me.
Mami smiles and tells her *thank you*
but I know I won't hear the end of it.

En casa ajena no se come.
No matter how much shit our stomach is talking.

As Christians we not supposed to lie
but as Mami's kids we not tryna get beat
for telling the truth.

Pero, maybe saying we not hungry
when we are is not a lie
if it serves a greater purpose, right?

Like, maybe God would be proud
that I said no to food I wanted.
Food I needed.

Jesus went through this too, right?
When he was fasting for forty days on the mountain
and the Devil came through and was like:

Ayo, you not hungry son?
Stop playin,' I know you can
turn them rocks into bread!

& Jesus was as calm as Mami is
in a face-to-face
at the welfare office

when her caseworkers wanna know
how much her job at the factory is paying
off the books so they can lower her food stamps.

& the story goes that Jesus broke character
and regulated on Satan real wild like:

Get thee behind me, Satan!!

I wonder if Mami ever wanted to break character
& tell her caseworkers to get behind her,

like really behind her & wait online for once
& see how it feels to watch your kids

beg for a life where they don't have to beg
for their life.

Get thee behind me, Satan!

And just like that Jesus chose to stay hungry
for a greater purpose.

Yo! Ain't it ironic that now we eat bread
to symbolize Jesus' body.

Damn, the Bible has like the weirdest plot twists.
Anyway, I think it's mad brave to believe

that one day your body
will be the only food you need.

But at Lala's house I didn't feel brave.
I felt hungry.

So maybe *bravery* is the wrong word for what I needed.
Maybe I needed faith. But first, I needed food.

HOOD CREDIT

So, check it. It goes like this. Goldo, the bodeguero, needs to make money to stay in business and Mami needs to feed Estrella & me. The relationship is a no-brainer. Trust is a huge part of this relationship. The bodeguero needs to trust Mami is gonna pay her tab when she gets paid and Mami needs to trust that the bodeguero won't suddenly switch up his borrowing policy in the middle of one of our hunger tantrums.

Fiao is a kind of credit that only has value in the hood. It's borrowing from the bodega when you ain't got no money. Just like a credit card or a loan from the bank if you think about it. Except the banks won't trust us to borrow money & the only card Mami got is the welfare card. But who needs any of that when you got Goldo? Next to Jesus, Goldo is the most revered saint on the block. Jesus feeds us spiritually and Goldo actually feeds us. *Fiao* is an unspoken pact to keep each other alive in a world that doesn't care if we die.

FIAO

Goldo could be a journalist too. He has a composition
notebook he writes in like me
except the only way you can guess the people's stories
is by looking at how much they owe.

Juan	~~$400.00~~	$200.00
Miguel		$ 32.50
Milagros		$125.00
Olga	$45.75	
Manuel	$249.00	

MAMI IS PREGNANT

Raffy is Mami's new boyfriend.
He has his own room.

Whenever Mami disappears
for hours, we know she's at Raffy's.

Raffy has suggested we all move in together
but Mami says she'll never live with a man again.

Mami & Raffy are having a baby
but we not supposed to know that.

Nobody tells us nothing around here,
which is fine, if they didn't act like we were stupid.

Being left out of conversations
means we start our own.

Being left out of conversations
just makes us more curious.

& being curious
means we go searching

for all the information
we not supposed to have.

BABY PICTURES

The assignment is to bring in a baby picture for a classroom game where everyone will guess who was who. Mami says I don't have baby pictures. We don't have any pictures at all. Mami couldn't afford to keep buying film, or she lost them all in a fire, or she is the fire, or she doesn't believe in remembering this life we live or looking back at kids she had from a man who did not love her.

GOD'S NOT DEAD
HE'S STILL ALIVE

Today Biggie died & our entire 8th-grade
homeroom is in mourning.

I say: *All of this crying for a rapper?*

Everybody in the class tells me I'm buggin'.
I gotta save face.

Aight chill, I know death is sad but come on—
It's not like we knew him—knew him.

Aight. The truth is I don't know Biggie's music.
Like. At all.

But it's wild embarrassing to admit
that there is only one radio in our apartment

that Mami insists belongs to Jesus.
Lala said I sounded mad dumb but she got me covered.

She's not tryna have me sounding stupid
in these streets. These are the kind of friends you need.

Friends who don't judge you
& instead talk shit about you to your face.

Lala got a dope Coby CD player with FM radio.
She stretches the headphones over both of our heads

until they almost break.
Biggie's lyrics vibrate through the flimsy ear covers.

We used to fuss when the landlord dissed us
No heat, wonder why Christmas missed us
Birthdays was the worst days
Now we sip Champagne when we thirsty
Uh, damn right, I like the life I live
'Cause I went from negative to positive

I watch my classmates dance, and cry at the same time.
The way Mami does when she catches the Holy Spirit.

My stomach does its own dance as I listen to a dead Biggie
rhyme about all of my deaths.

Maybe this is how Mami feels
when she listens to her Jesus radio.

I bet if my homegirl's CD player belonged to a god
it would be Biggie.

Biggie is dead.
Jesus is dead.

& somehow they are both still alive.

HOTEL, MOTEL, HOLIDAY INN

The church passed a collection plate around
so we have enough money to stay in a motel
for a couple of weeks.

Estrella says motels are dirty.
It's where girls convince
stupid lonely guys to pay them for sex.

How do you know this stuff? I ask her, mad suspicious.
I hear shit. Damn. What you tryna say?

We crack up and inhale the secondhand smoke
seeping through the door

while Mami splashes olive oil on the walls
to protect us from evil.

On one side of the wall
a woman screams at God in pleasure or pain.

On the other side of the wall
Mami screams at God.

WOMEN, INFANTS & CHILDREN

Mami gets a check once a month
that she can trade in the store for food.

We can't trade it for Chinese food,
cuchifritos or Taco Bell though, which is wack.

WIC vouchers look like a real check
& you actually have to sign for your food

and show ID, I guess to make sure
no one else is tryna steal your poor-ass identity.

I think if someone is tryna steal
Mami's WIC check
they must need it more than us.

Anyway, instead of a dollar amount
the check shows you the type of food,

how much food and even the name brand
of food you are allowed to get.

There is usually no way around this.
Goldo could risk losing his license

if he was caught allowing us
to get things that are not on the list.

But sometimes we swap the Juicy Juice
for some 7-Up and Goldo acts

like he didn't see shit.

HOW WE GOT OUR NAMES
TROPICAL FANTASY

I cop the pineapple Tropical Fantasy & Estrella says
they put these drinks in our hoods to kill us.

Think about it. You ever see Tropical Fantasy
in white people stores?

I ain't never been to no white people store
so how am I supposed to know what they drink?

I roll my eyes at Estrella and drink it anyway.
'cause if the soda doesn't kill me the thirst will.

Plus, I kind of like saying that I'm going to the store
to buy a Tropical Fantasy.

As if I can finally afford something
that I wasn't supposed to.

SIDE HUSTLE

I didn't even get to enjoy my Tropical Fantasy
when I peep Mami running down Knickerbocker Avenue.

Raffy don't see her
about to charge him.

He is too busy screaming *Tempooooo.*
Tempooooo para las cucarachas. Tempoooo.

Mami's hands catch up with Raffy
before her body does.

She slaps Raffy per syllable.
SIN-VER-GÜEN-ZA. MAL-PA-RI-DO.

She ends with a two-syllable punch *CA-BRÓN*
before he grabs her wrists and stops her.

Mami has been giving Raffy train money
so he could go to the city and search for a job

& here he is using it to buy & flip
roach poison in the hood.

Mami is yelling so loud
I think she might give birth.

Yo aquí matándome y estas muchachas con hambre
& you can't even find a real job. Canto estúpido.

Raffy yells back that this is a real job.
& pulls out mad wrinkled dollars from his socks.

Mami rips the money from his hands and gives it to me.
Sarai, go order a pepperoni pie and get a two-liter 7-Up.

I feel bad for Mami & Raffy.
Worried about where they gonna get the next dollar.

But I can't be worried
about adult problems.

'Cause tonight we eating good.
        Tonight we eating good.

LEAVE BEFORE YOU'RE LEFT

Back at the motel Mami picks up Estrella
& my clothes from the floor

& stuffs them into black garbage bags.
We don't own no suitcases or book bags.

Just a shopping cart and
some 99 cents bootleg Heftys.

She says we going back to the church
before Raffy comes by looking for her.

She don't wanna be around no man
that lies to her.

She wants to shake him up a little bit.
Make him worry about her.

Make him regret treating her like a fool.
He got too comfortable. Like all men do

when they get a good thing going.

Better to leave than to be left.
Even Jesus knew that.

Look how loyal we are to him now.
Look how much we appreciate him now.

Look how we ask for forgiveness.
& wait for him to come back.

HOW WE GOT OUR NAMES
ANGRY BITCHES

Sarai, don't ever trust a man with the truth, Mami said.
They only want lies. Fantasías.

Things that make them feel good
even if it makes you feel bad.

Like the time Mami gave herself the gift of being glass,
and Papi only saw her shards.

Now every time I see Papi, I practice smiling.
If I ever have to cry around him,

I make sure it sounds like laughter.
Pero of course, I know how to be multiple things at once.

I come from a woman who prays like she's fighting.
I come from a woman who will burn her hands

for you to have a hot meal
but will tell you to serve yourself.

I come from a woman so passionate
the world calls her angry.

Maybe Mami's not angry.
Maybe she just knows what she's worth.

EL BODEGUERO

Toward the end of the month
Mami has racked up so much credit

that Goldo doesn't allow her to borrow anything else
until she's paid off what she owes.

I thought Goldo was an asshole for that
until this weekend, when Papi decides

to be a really good father and buys us
salami and cheese sandwiches.

Goldo tells Papi that he's glad Papi comes around
and buys us food because he worries

about us being hungry all the time
but doesn't wanna let Mami borrow so much

that she spends all her money paying him back
and can't afford to buy us anything else.

I look at the cruel man with the stocked shelves
and then at my new jelly sandals

Mami got us from Payless &
I decide to gift him a forgiving smile

but he can't smile back.
Papi's hands are already around his neck

like a microphone he is yelling into
his voice echoing to the whole store

that he always makes sure his kids are good
and that the next time Goldo decides
not to mind his business

he might not have a business to mind.

GOOD JOBS
BAD JOBS

Papi is a carpenter at a woodworking factory
on Hart Street.

He makes custom furniture
for la gente rica in Manhattan.

Hart Street is one of the nicer blocks
in Bushwick

where people own their houses
and the grass isn't so littered

with dope baggies.
Mami says Papi only got a job that good

because he blends in with the gringos.
I think of Welo and remember what Wela said.

Papi es un blanco Puerto Rican.
Papi and his green eyes could pass

for Irish, maybe Italian,
as long as he didn't open his mouth.

Mami told me Raffy tried to get a job there
but was told he just didn't have the look

to lock in big furniture contracts,
which I think means he was too brown.

Papi thinks it's ridiculous
to blame his light eyes and skin

for him having a good job. He's worked hard to be
where he's at.

Doesn't matter what color you are or where you're from.
Just work hard & you'll make it, he says.

Just work hard and you'll make it.

ERASURE

I'm thinking about why
we don't talk about color.

I remember once in art class
we talked about how the color white

is actually composed
of many different colors.

But no one ever talks about that
so it ends up that the color white

gets its clout in the
absence of the other colors.

In other words
white needs the other colors to simply exist

but those other colors never
get any credit.

Unless you start doing research
or pay attention in art class you'd

never know they're even there.
Makes you wonder

if white is even a color at all
if it can only exist when

all of the other colors
are erased.

HOW WE GOT OUR NAMES
FIVE DOLLAR SHOE STORE

The first of the month is here
and that's when Mami has the most money.

A new shoe store opened up
on Knickerbocker Avenue and everyone's hype.

Unlike Payless, which is quickly becoming Paymore,
the Five Dollar Shoe Store lets us know exactly how

much we gotta sacrifice out of our food budget
for a new pair of kicks.

I ain't never seen something
named so honestly.

PORK-FRIED RICE MONEY

If Mami has some money left over after we pay Goldo
we walk over to the Chinos on Knickerbocker.

Mami lets us get whatever we want.
I always order an egg roll, dollar fries with extra ketchup
& barbecue sauce.

Mami gets the beef and broccoli
just so we can have some vegetables.

If she's in a good mood
we get to eat our food at the restaurant

and for a moment everybody on the block
can see us living good

through the clear glass windows. There are mirrors
on the walls and I take advantage of seeing myself happy.

My mouth slick with grease.
My lips, full and glossed.

HOW WE GOT OUR NAMES
DANNY

My brother Danny used to live with Mami.
When Papi left, Mami said she noticed

Danny needed more help
than she could give him.

He couldn't keep
moving from place to place with us.

So now he lives in a home
for people with disabilities.

Mami says this is temporary.
Until we get on our feet.

Now we visit him every Saturday
at a place where the furniture is bolted to the floor.

We wait for the 13 bus on Myrtle Avenue
then ride it to the last stop,

where the grass is so green it tricks you
into thinking you've left New York.

There is a merry-go-round in the middle
of the trickster field,

so colorful you almost forget
how sad the whole story is.

VISITING DANNY AT THE GROUP HOME

Danny yells out Estrella's name when he sees me.
He can't pronounce it fully so he says Lela.

I don't tell him I'm Sarai
because I know it makes him feel good

to recognize someone he grew up with.
Estrella can't come 'cuz Mami can only afford

one bus token for herself & since I'm short
I duck a little bit & get on the bus for free.

I get on first 'cause we never know how the bus driver
is gonna react to me tryna get over on the fare.

If the bus driver is in a good mood he'll let it slide.
If the bus driver is in a bad mood he'll kick us out

& we'll wait for the next bus
& start all over again.

Danny doesn't know me.
& I don't know him.

He went to live at the home before either of us
could form memories of each other.

He talks differently than we do. He slurs his words,
& sounds like he's talking in slow motion.

Danny can say our names
and ask for junk food.

We are always ready with
Cheez Doodles, Devil Dogs & quarter juices.

ANTONIO

At the bodega while paying the rest of what she owed
to Goldo, Mami met this dude named Antonio.

He said to call him Tone.
Tone must have reminded her of God

or something because suddenly she started speaking
like she does when she's praying.

She told Tone about where we live and don't live,
what we eat and don't eat.

About Raffy cogiéndola de pendeja.
& Tone being "the savior" that Mami

guessed him to be, said that he has an extra bedroom
in his three-bedroom apartment on Troutman Street

and that we could stay there
as long as we needed to.

All she had to do was give him half the rent:
two hundred dollars a month.

Mami said *Gracias a Dios* even though she meant
Gracias a Antonio. She apologized as she told Goldo

that she'd only be paying half of her balance today.
I'm excited at the thought of having a permanent place to live.

A home that lets me get to know it long enough
to give me something to write about.

THE APARTMENT ON TROUTMAN STREET

Tone's apartment is on Troutman & Irving.
The hottest block in Bushwick.
We move in at night so no one asks any questions.
Tone says the front door is always broken
so we don't need keys.

The new crib is on the 3rd floor.
Some stairs are missing and the railing
wiggles like a tooth that's about to fall out ya mouth.
The hallway smells like something died here.

The R.I.P. tags on the walls
lets me know that someone did.
On the door a sticker that says *3R* is peeling off.
Struggling like everything else.

The door got mad locks and Tone struggles
to push it open. It fights against newspapers,
and boxes stacked on each other behind the door.

Inside, I flick the light switch and nothing happens.
Tone says he's working on the light bill
and grabs a flashlight from a crate.

The light dances over more crates full of hammers
and drills and tools I can't name.
I scan the rooms with the flashlight
like I'm investigating a crime scene.

The entire apartment looks like a repair shop.
TVs with no backs, radios with no dial buttons,
busted speakers, fans with wires blowing out of them.

I almost slip on some batteries.
A few rusty cans with brown water in them
are scattered all over the floor.
Estrella & I spot an intact TV.

Tone says it works
& we can have it.
It's the first thing we move into our new room.
We argue about what show we're gonna watch first.

She wants to watch the baby mama drama
on *Ricki Lake* but I wanna watch the news
which I'm sure will be better than a talk show

'cause the drama is always us.

THE NEWS SAYS BUSHWICK HAS A DRUG PROBLEM

but I don't see anybody trying to fix it.
If they were, I wouldn't have to skip over Julie
in our new hallway.

I'm so careful not to wake her up.
She looks like she found a peace
most of us haven't yet.

Sometimes, when I am trying to beat the rats
to the front door, Julie shrieks and jumps up.

I know this means I'll be late to school
'cause Julie makes me stand in front of her.

She fixes my hair and clothes and commands me
in a voice that sounds like regret to stay in school.

She has me make promises to her on the spot.
Promise that I won't be like her.

Promise that I'll bring her some food
if I have any left over from lunch, even if it's an apple,

she's cool with just an apple.
She stay asking for food

even though when I come back
home with it she's gone.

It makes me wonder if she remembers
what she asked me for or if she just wants

to be on someone's mind throughout the day.
She stands in front of me like I am her reflection.

She tells me I am so, so beautiful
and since I am her mirror
I tell her that she's beautiful back.

PLANNING

It's April & it looks like it's about to pour.
I'm chillin' with Estrella & Lala on our new stoop.

We're discussing plans to make it out the hood.
Lala & I think getting good jobs is the move.

Look at Ms. Rivera. She's getting paid now, I say.
& giving back to her community.

Estrella laughs.
Ms. Rivera probably don't even like her job.

& you know she's still broke
'cuz her acrylics stay chipped.

Estrella says teachers don't get paid
what we think they get paid.

& who is gonna hire Puerto Ricans
from Bushwick and pay them enough to get outta here?

Lala says that all we gotta do is get good grades
& go to college and we can make a good living.

I agree. Yo. *All we gotta do is prove*
that we can be just as good as anybody else.

Yo. Better.

Estrella says she's not proving shit to nobody.
& the sky roars as she's talking

like a warning or a cheer depending
on who is listening to the story.

G

My neighbor G in apartment 3L sells drugs
out of his apartment.

The crackheads always think our door is the one
with the magic. They leave their wands on the stairs.

& Estrella and I take turns kicking the crack stems
out the way with our new Five Dollar Shoe Store kicks.

I wonder which one of these belongs to Julie.

TO STEAL OR NOT TO STEAL

Estrella came home with mad money today.
She gave Mami some for the light bill.

& bought me my own Coby CD player
with FM radio!

Estrella knows I been sneak switching
Mami's radio to La Mega 97.9 FM when she's asleep

ever since I learned that salsa music
is exactly like Pentecostal music

but with better storytelling.
How could you afford this?

She said she found somebody's wallet
on the floor of Goldo's bodega.

She took the money but returned the wallet
with all the IDs and shit 'cause she's not that foul.

Isn't that still stealing, though?
Now we're taking stolen money?

Mami searches the drawer for the light bill.

Give me back your CD player then
Since you so holy. I'll give it to somebody who's grateful.

But I don't give it back.
& Mami doesn't give back the light bill money.

'Cause if we did
Estrella would still be a thief.

& our lights would never come back on.
& somebody else would get to listen to salsa.

A REAL G

Estrella and I giggle as we run past G
who is holding a shotgun in the hallway.

We take turns teasing, asking G what his real name is.
Gustavo, George, Gabriel, Giovanni?

A gold chain hangs a single glimmering letter g
from his neck. Maybe *G* is not the initial to his name.

Maybe g is short for *giant, gospel* or *gangsta*.
Even though we've already seen it,

g hides his gun behind his back
and yells at us to get back in the apartment.

Inside, we take turns watching G from the peephole.
He paces up and down the hallway, shotgun by his side.

Like a real G. A soldier protecting his castle.

911 WHAT'S YOUR EMERGENCY

There is a shootout.

The bullets are flying

across our

rooftops.

Since our beds are by the windows,

we slide onto the floor

and the floor slides into us.

The splinters in our hands & knees

are a small price to pay

for avoiding an accidental bullet.

Mami tells me to call the cops

so she doesn't have to.

Calling the cops is a dangerous activity

on multiple levels.

If the dealers don't punish you for it

there's a possibility the cops will.

The cops are real reckless with their guns.

Sometimes as reckless as the dealers.

The news reports them shooting somebody in the hood

on what seems like a regular basis.

It's almost as if the cops have their own gang.

The 911 operator hangs up

& we wait

For the bullets to stop.

For the cops to arrive.

For the morning to lend us enough light

to remove the splinters

from our bodies

like small wooden trophies.

THIS IS THE DAY THAT THE LORD HAS MADE LET US REJOICE & BE GLAD IN IT

It's Sunday morning and we are still alive.
The cops never came through last night

but here they are knocking on our door at 9 a.m.
looking like they got some good sleep.

Mami said not to open the door.
We might have known something last night

but we don't know nothing now.
Through the peephole I can see

the ceiling lights flicker
& the cops lean against the yellow-brown walls

palms steady
resting on their guns

like small steel trophies.

YOUR SILENCE WILL NOT PROTECT YOU

The news only reports on our deaths when

we demand to be heard.

That's how come we got to be so loud, I think.

So people know we in danger if we ever get too quiet.

TODAY IN BIBLE STUDY

Now faith is the assurance of things hoped for,
the conviction of things not seen.

Faith is mad simple to explain but harder to execute.
The pastor says we should trust that God will provide

what we need even when we can't possibly see how.
Not all of us possess faith.

The pastor says the corner boys
don't have faith that God will provide, so they sell drugs.

They put their faith in crack, heroin & people who use
them.
Estrella gives an example to see if she gets it:

Oh, like last winter when the heat didn't come up,
& we prayed for the radiator to work but it didn't,

so we put our faith in our coats?
How does this trick work again?

Everyone thinks Estrella is being a smart-ass
but I know Estrella is just being smart.

WE DON'T KNOW WHO THE LANDLORD IS BUT WE KNOW HE DON'T CARE

Don't care about the rats
racing us to the door.
Don't care about the roof & the rain's
collaboration to drown us.
Don't care about the splitting floor
and its stabbing ways.
Don't care about the front door
locks that stay broken.
Don't care about the bucket
we use for a toilet.
Don't care about the chipped walls
underneath our nails.
Don't care about the stairs
missing steps or the wobbly railing.
Don't care about the coldest radiator ever.
Don't care about the missing light bulbs in the hallway.
Don't care about the crack pipes
or the syringes by our door.
The Landlord cares about the rent.
Tone says the Landlord will evict us if we can't pay it.
Which means we may be the only garbage
he's willing to throw out.

THE CORNER BOYS

Today, the cops arrested Corner Boy Jesus.
Estrella was chilling with them when twelve rolled up.

She said he wasn't even doing nothing
but doing nothing around here always means trouble.

Doing nothing around here means you don't care
enough to do something

which means you must want to die.
In this neighborhood, if you don't want to die

you got to do something.
Even the cops know this.

That's why they took in one of the corner boys.
So they can say they did something.

So the corner boys don't try to do something.
& this is how everybody stays alive.

MY LIFE AS A BIBLE STORY
DAVID & GOLIATH

Around here, drugs have names too.
     Dust, Perico, Manteca, Snow, Coca.

G sells Goliath.
  I realize that maybe G never went to Bible study.

Maybe if he knew how wack Goliath actually was
he wouldn't sell it on the block.

    I decide to mind my business & act like
I don't know that he's talking about selling drugs.

  I pretend to be mad excited
   'cuz David & Goliath is my favorite Bible story.

Ayo, G, ain't it wild how David beat Goliath?!
Even though Goliath was a giant. Like way bigger than David.

Goliath was such a punk.
Who gets beaten by a pebble?

G looks stunned & changes the subject.
Says to let him know what we need to eat.

G sometimes hooks the building up with compra.
I say we ran out of corned beef.

I hear G tell the corner boys
to go to Associated & cop us some corned beef

                    & to let everyone know that he's not selling
Goliath no more
                            but he got mad pebbles on deck.

Yo, ain't that a trip?
Here I was trying to make G stop selling
& all I did was help him market it better.

I gotta be more careful with my mouth.
It's more powerful than I think.

CAREER DAY

I know the school year is almost over
when Career Day comes through

to get us thinking about our future
outside of Bushwick.

Futures with doctors and lawyers.
Not a job or a side hustle. A career.

A career is your identity
& your identity is something you keep.

The teachers say Career Day
gets us ready for the real world.
Lala jokes: *Does that mean our world is fake?*

The class is wilin' again. *Yoooo!*
What if we was made up by somebody?

It's not so far-fetched.
Estrella and I make up worlds when we play Barbies.

Anyways, if we *are* just a game
that somebody in the real world
is playing I wish they'd hurry up
and tell me if I win or lose.

IN LIVING COLOR

Some days Lala & I play hooky
when Lala's mom takes an extra shift at the

hospital. Lala locks the door & digs in her pocket
for the wrinkled paper with the number to the chat line.

On the chat line I don't have to wear loose floral skirts
to avoid unwanted attention.

On the chatline we are as safe and gorgeous as we wanna be.
We giggle and take turns lying to boys

about our age, height and where we live.
Since there is only one jack, only one of us

gets to be beautiful at a time.
In between turns we watch reruns

of our favorite show
and decide on who we'll be next.

Today, Lala is Jennifer Lopez, a fly girl
from the Bronx.

I am Rosie Perez 'cause she's from Bushwick
& sounds just like me.

ESTRELLA WANTS TO GET PAID TO HAVE SEX

Estrella likes to shock people so they pay attention
to her but today she sounds serious.

Think about it. She explains.
You basically just have sex with men,

which we're eventually gonna do anyway,
so we might as well get paid for it.

Right?

Women who have sex for free are dumb.

She won't even need a pimp.

Why give your money to a man
when you did all the work?

& when Jesus gets out of jail he could get her a burner.
Just in case she gotta protect herself.

Anyway, she thinks women who have sex for money
get a bad rep.

Why can't that be a career too?

Mami has a name for women
who sell their bodies: sucias.

Estrella argues that would make the men
who pay for sex dirty too.

But the pastor says the men who buy sex have a sickness.
Just like people who are addicted to drugs,

& we should pray for them.
But who prays for the dealers? Estrella says.

Who prays for the women?

PRAYER

Mami just got fired from her job
at the sewing factory on Dekalb Ave.

She came home yelling about the bosses
being *un bonche racistas, sucios y malos*.

So maybe Papi doesn't know what he's talking about.
Mami worked hard and it didn't matter.

All those days putting up
with the way they talked to her

like she wasn't worth
the machine she worked on.

Ms. Rivera once said that
words are usually a red carpet for actions.

All Mami did was ask to come in late
so she could go to her prenatal appointment.

They told her maybe she should prioritize her pregnancy
and come back when she didn't need so much time off.

Now Mami spends all her days crying
and looking for a new job.

Crying and looking for a new job.
I'm glad Mami & Raffy

have been working on their issues
so he can take the job of making her feel better.

Raffy says it's bad for the baby to be so stressed
and says maybe Mami should talk to someone.

Mami talks to God, she says.
Anybody who has serious problems talks to God.

I decide tonight I'm gonna talk to God.

HOW MAMI LOST THE BABY

Everything happened so fast.
In the middle of the night we heard Mami scream

that she was bleeding. I thought she was tryna say
that we ran out of toilet paper

since that's what we use
when we get our period

and when we run out we gotta
cut up rags from T-shirts

& then Estrella & I get into an argument
about whose T-shirt is worth saving.

But Mami didn't ask for toilet paper.
She asked us to call 911.

911 for a period is dramatic, no?
Estrella calls me stupid

for not knowing bleeding is a dangerous sign
for a pregnant woman.

The ambulance took forever to come.
Then the doctor took forever to come.
Then Raffy took forever to come.

The last thing that arrived
is usually always the first:

bad news.

Mami lost the baby.

GOOD DAYS

Things have been real quiet around here
since Mami's miscarriage.

Mami spends most of her days cleaning,
praying and reading the Bible.

I know she's hurt but we never see her cry.
I usually do my crying in the shower

so nobody asks me any questions.
Maybe Mami is a shower crier like me.

Today, Danny is having dinner with us.
Mami said Danny would be staying with us for a few days.

The group home allowed it since Tone is never home.
Mami lied and told them it was our apartment.

We've been eating so good lately
'cause Raffy started hustling

bootleg VHSs on Knickerbocker Avenue
and stops by with cash.

& Estrella keeps coming home with random money.
Tonight we're having white rice, eggs and corned beef

with red beans on the side. Mami even added potatoes
and onions to the corned beef!

I hate onions so I take them out,
but onions are a sign it's a good food day.

Estrella flings the ketchup packets we steal from school
and tries to land them between the goal post

I've made with my hands.

Danny yells at Estrella like he wants to play too while
Mami carefully wipes leftover food from Danny's mouth.

I've never seen her hands touch any of us like that.
She looks mad happy, yo. Today we're mad happy, yo.

I can count these moments on one hand
but maybe I'll need a new hand soon.

KUMBAYA

Danny is taking a nap
& Mami shoots Estrella & me a warning

to keep it down.
Danny has mad energy.

Mami spends most of hers
running around after him.

That could be stressful
but these days I haven't heard her complain once.

She seems so happy lately.
Like she found peace.

She even asks us what we want to eat.
Like Lala's mom does.

It's weird.
It's like she's normal.

Estrella & I don't ask questions
'cause we don't wanna jinx it.

But we shoot each other WTF stares
whenever Mami helps Danny get dressed

or suggests we should sing
a corito together as a family.

It's like we're in some weird Christian camp
and Mami is the suspiciously nice camp counselor

who has a secret
we can't quite figure out.

PROFESSIONAL SPANISH KNOCKS ON THE DOOR

At first we don't answer.
Knocks that loud usually mean 5-0 is on the other end.

> *Señora, ábrenos la puerta por favor.*
> *Estamos aquí para platicar con usted.*
> *No queremos llamar la policía.*

The person on the other side of the door
is speaking professional Spanish.

Professional Spanish is fake friendly.
Is a warning.

Is a downpour when you
just spent your last $20 on a wash and set.

Is the kind of Spanish that comes
to take things away from you.

The kind of Spanish that looks at your Spanish
like it needs help.

Professional Spanish of course doesn't offer help.
It just wants you to know that it knows you need some.

Professional Spanish is stuck-up
like most people from the hood who get good jobs.

Professional Spanish is all like
I did it, you can do it too.

Professional Spanish thinks
it gets treated better than us

because it knows how to follow the rules.
Because it says *abrigo* instead of *có*.

Because it knows which fork belongs to the salad
and which spoon goes in the coffee.

Because it gets to be the anchor
on Telemundo and Univision

and we get to be the news
that plays behind its head in the background.

DANNY IS KIDNAPPED

Before we can stop him
Danny opens the door for the people

speaking professional Spanish.
Two cops immediately grab Danny

by his arms and wrists as if
he were under arrest.

Professional Spanish lady tries to restrain Mami,
who's yelling at the men to let go of Danny.

Everybody is screaming
but nobody is saying anything.

What's going on?

I don't know if Estrella wants to help
or is just being nosy.

Your mother violated her visitation rights.
Danny was supposed to be back at the group home two days ago.

Mami is still screaming like she's wounded
and someone ripped the Band-Aid off.

In this case if happiness is the Band-Aid,
then the wound is losing another kid so soon.

BUSHWICK LIBRARY

Mami has started dropping Estrella & me off at the library
every Saturday.

If there wasn't a time limit on how long you can neglect
your kids before it becomes abandon,

maaaaan, Mami would leave us there 'til Sunday.

The library gives Mami a vacation from us.
For one day she gets to live inside of a world

where she doesn't have to be someone's mother.
A miracle even Jesus would be proud of.

& maybe that makes her sound like a bad mom—
but I love Mami for this 'cause for one day

we get to live inside of a book
and be somebody else too.

BOOKS WE READ

The neighborhoods in the books we read
have nice houses.

The houses in the books we read
don't have rats & roaches.

The rats & roaches in the books we read
are cute, magical and friendly.

The friends in the books we read
come from rich families.

The families in the books we read
communicate with words.

The words in the books we read
don't curse.

The curses in the books we read
are broken with love.

The love in the books we read
always wins.

Winning is always how the story ends.
The end of the story means we return to real life.

YOU GOT POTENTIAL

I am supposed to be someone. Someday.
If I really want to be. If I keep my grades up.

That's what my teachers keep telling me.
My potential is something they like to throw in my face.

They use that word like it's a gift that I won't open or
some shit.
They say that I can be or do anything I want.

They say that like they almost believe it.
Pero, like, what exactly do they mean

I could be someone if I really wanted to?
So, who do they think I am now?

ASK ME ANYTHING DAY
WITH MS. RIVERA

Today we learned Ms. Rivera still lives in the hood.
Her hood is in the Bronx. That's where Papi lives.
I've never visited. We really don't leave the block.
Also, the Bronx sounds mad far.
Ms. Rivera said Puerto Ricans live there as well.
She said the Bronx is where hip-hop was born.
Some say it's where salsa was born too.
She said the music we bop to was birthed by all of us.
I look around. All of us are Puerto Rican, Black American,
Dominican, Mexican, Ecuadorian, Salvadorian.
Man, all of us are everything except White American.
I wonder where they go to school?
I look around and remember how we danced
in homeroom when Biggie died.
Lala's sleepover with the Spice Girls.
Our Pentecostal coritos and all the tunes
I sneak listen to on hot 97.
The thought of us birthing music makes me smile.
I tell Lala that I think it's cool to know
that we could give birth to something
other than babies. 'Cause I heard having a baby hurts.
Lala agrees that it's real cool to know
that we could give birth to something other than pain.

MY LIFE AS A SALSA SONG
LA VIDA TE DA SORPRESAS

I take advantage of Ask Me Anything Day
and try and find out how much Ms. Rivera gets paid.

Ayo, Miss. How you make all this money
and still live in the hood?

Ms. Rivera laughs
and says: *What money? Where?*

She then adds that not everybody
can leave the hood & also not everybody

wants to leave the hood.
& that's news to me.

       Maaaan.
That's news to me.

CODE SWITCH

I'm learning new words
so that I can sprinkle them

in between the old words.
Like if I say my life is not off
to a very auspicious start.

I mean or I think I mean
that shit is wild in Bushwick.

One day if I ever write a book
I'll use that word in a way
that makes more sense.

A book where all the new words
will be next to all the old words

Each   one   brilliant   and   mattering.

NEW WORDS/IRONIC/
SOMETHING THAT IS EXACTLY THE OPPOSITE OF WHAT IS MEANT OR EXPECTED TO HAPPEN

Today Lala & I decide to see if
Papo is posted up with his carrito

inside Maria Hernandez Park
so we can buy some beaded necklaces from him for the
parade.

Maria Hernandez was shot
through her window in 1989.

Maria and her husband were known
for tryna clean up Bushwick.

They were supposed to be the heroes
in the story of The War on Drugs.

The newspapers reported
that she was revenge murdered by local drug dealers.

Today the park where all the people who get high sleep
& all the dealers deal

is named after her.

NEW WORDS/PRESERVATION/
TO KEEP ALIVE OR IN EXISTENCE

Everything in Bushwick lasts longer than it needs to.

Preservation is a skill you learn in the hood.

We do things Bill Nye the Science Guy would

be proud of: keep butter containers to store our food,

use old clothes for rags.

Even the way people love

in the hood has to be built to last.

Love in the hood is a kind of loyalty

to your own survival.

Everyone lived by this, even Maria.

Even the dealers who killed her.

HOW WE GOT OUR NAMES
NEIGHBORHOOD WATCH

When our parents don't help us.
We blame Mami & Papi for not loving us enough.

When the banks don't help us.
We blame jobs for not hiring us enough.

When the schools don't help us.
We blame ourselves for not learning enough.

When the hospitals don't help us.
We blame the medicines for not working enough.

When the church don't help us.
We blame God for not listening enough.

When the cops don't help us.
We blame ourselves & start policing each other.

                                    We don't help us.

Only we help us.

116TH STREET FESTIVAL

It's the second Saturday in June. The Puerto Rican Day Parade is tomorrow but everybody knows that the festival is where we get to shine. Lala and I are decked out head to toe in the flag but it's not enough so we find Papo who is selling Puerto Rican flag necklaces out of a shopping cart and we just know we gotta have one. Two! Three? No, that's too much. Oh! Snap! Papo got whistles and bandanas?! We're copping that too! Lala buys a top hat striped with the flag that kind of makes her look like a Puerto Rican Mad Hatter. We bop down the streets like we're trying to prove something to somebody. We stop to watch a couple of OGs dance to El Gran Combo's "Un Verano en Nueva York." We can't dance salsa so Lala and I clap and lean our bodies toward the boombox. The dancing couple nods our way, a salute to the way Lala and I wave our flag-drenched bodies towards their swing. The woman grabs her long skirt, a flag of her own, and waves it back toward us. I don't know if it was the long skirt or if it was the way she seemed to be possessed by some spirit, holy or other, but for a second the woman turns into Mami & it's so good to see her dancing & not worrying about bills or food. It's so good to see a crowd around her as if she were a god we all gathered to worship. I clap a little harder than I would at church. Excited to see the possibility of freedom right in front of me. This is the rapture I wait for.

QUÉ BONITA BANDERA

Señor Maví peeps Lala and me getting ready
to head down to the Puerto Rican Day Parade

on Knickerbocker Avenue.

¡Mira! Qué chévere.
¡Boricua hasta el fin!

¿Pero qué saben
ustedes de Puerto Rico?

Lala and I don't answer
partly because we're insulted

and partly because he's right;
we don't really know shit about Puerto Rico.

Señor Maví shakes his head
like he's disappointed.

He says that we need to learn our history
because the flag we're waving means something.

Había un tiempo en cual la ley
prohibía hasta tener una bandera.

I can't imagine the Puerto Rican flag
ever having been illegal to own.

Ay. Mister. That was a long time ago, Lala says, annoyed.
You can't be stuck in the past, Señor. Where's your flag?

Señor Maví tips his brown felt brimmed hat,
taps the one pocket on the left side
of his white button-down shirt.

My fla' is hea'.
He says, in an English that doesn't pronounce the g in flag.

My fla' is hea'.

THE PUERTO RICAN DAY PARADE ON KNICKERBOCKER AVENUE

The Puerto Rican Day Parade on Knickerbocker Avenue is
the unofficial official parade 'cause it takes place on

our turf & on our terms.

The police try and shut the parade down
every year 'cause dique we don't got no permit to gather

but Puerto Ricans know asking for permission never got
us nowhere & so we just celebrate now & worry

about the consequences later. Lala and I make our way
through the crowd starting at Circo's Bakery & walk

seven blocks all the way to Tony's Pizza.
Lala & I point out things to each other

making sure we don't miss anything
like the adorable toddler representing

with the Boricua T-shirt
sitting curiously on her mother's shoulders.

Or the lady selling cheese, beef & chicken empanadas.
Or the cops who are having a good time

but don't wanna show it.
Move it along. Move it along.

The domino tables and oversized speakers
on the side streets where the dancing happens.

The cars block the streets and you can't tell
if the horns honking are Puerto Ricans

or people telling Puerto Ricans to get out of the way.
I wonder if Señor Maví would say this is history.

I decide it is.
I decide it is.

WE MAKE THE NEWS

Tonight, I switched through all the channels to look for
Lala and her Puerto Rican Mad Hatter hat

or Papo and his carrito, or the OG couple dancing,
or the representing-ass toddler.

Instead, people are asking the mayor to pass new laws
that would stop the parade.

We get together and they call us a mob.
We laugh and they call it a riot.

Next week, I'll be the first person
to graduate 8th grade in my family.

That's history in somebody's books. No?
That's worthy of making the news. No?

But nothing good we do makes the news.
        Nothing good we do makes the news.

THE MAYOR SAYS:
I DON'T THINK YOUTH
PROGRAMS WILL HELP

because he says we are hardened criminals
who are all in gangs and need jail, not sewing lessons.

Lala, Estrella & I are on the stoop laughing
at the latest bochinche on the news.

Why the hell would we want sewing lessons?
I think of Mami & her job at la factoría.

I mean, maybe you could sew yourself some pants.
Lala chimes in with the Pentecostal jokes.

The mayor wouldn't survive one day
in the hood. Estrella sucks her teeth hard.

Julie stumbles out of the hallway
to tell us that she's trying to sleep

& we're too loud.

IF YOU CARE TO LOOK CLOSELY

the war on drugs

is also a war on people.

But in Bushwick,

no one cares to look closely.

THE WAR ON ROACHES

The roaches wear our clothes and eat our bootleg
Lucky Charms.

They hitch rides in our fake JanSports
& embarrass us in school.

They have meetings when we're asleep
about how they're going to take over.

At night they gather in the kitchen by the hundreds
but I suspect there could be thousands of them.

I only know 'cause one time I turned on the light
and caught them marching

like they were in a parade
no one could shut down.

GRADUATION DAY

Today, I am the first person
to graduate the 8th grade in my family.

I almost didn't. Last week, I got into a fight
with a girl ironically named Dulce.

I caught Dulce staring at me. I don't really know why
but you're not supposed to let people look at you

for too long. If you let them keep staring
who knows what else they'll try to get away with.

What are you looking at?
is always a fair warning shot before the fists.

A chance for them to look away or explain themselves.
A chance for you to be unseen.

Remain hidden to someone
who might have noticed too much about you.

Like that you're wearing Payless sneakers
or that you might be homeless.

The Bible says you're supposed to
turn the other cheek

but Dulce must have missed that verse
and punched me in both

before I even had the chance to offer one.
All I could do was swing like I was trying to fly away

maybe back to some heaven
before I learned the anger in my hands.

Mami was furious when she got the call
& had to beg the school to let me graduate.

She couldn't afford the bus fare to see me
walk across the stage.

But I accept my diploma
in honor of the fight Mami won.

MY LIFE AS A SALSA SONG
UN VERANO EN NUEVA YORK

I know school is out and it's summertime when the
corner of the block is peppered with old men massag-
ing their domino tables like they're apologizing to their
side chicks for being gone for so long while the block
DJ sits one leg out the driver's side of his Honda Civic
blasting old music through a duct-taped window 'cause
all the new hip-hop sucks except for maybe Jay-Z and
maybe a few of those new Marc Anthony joints but
only 'cause he's basically a legend though he's no Fania
All-Star or nothing pero everybody knows if you stick
around long enough and refuse to leave what you love
basically becomes something you can't let go of which
is why Mami left Papi 'cause you can love something
until you die but that doesn't mean you have to let it
kill you around here all of us play like we are safe even
when we are not we run nowhere and everywhere &
damn it feels like we could take over anything it feels
like we own this place everyone has forgotten and is

trying to leave so maybe being Puerto Rican means you some kind of legendary because you are the product of what happens when two people leave the island and make love in an abandoned apartment building in Brooklyn but not so abandoned that they can't live there just abandoned enough to be ignored by everyone but the sun blasting through the broken window like a song.

ESTRELLA GOT PLANS TO MAKE IT OUT

On the first day of summer
Estrella spills her body
    all over the stoop
so it remembers her
  when she leaves.

She's dyed her hair red
& it looks like a dying sunset or
one of them Bushwick fires Señor Maví told us about.
I laugh and frown at the visuals in my head.

Estrella tells me to fix my face.
   Around here we gotta walk around with the ice grill
so nobody will try to talk to us. I hear Papi's voice.
Men don't like angry bitches.

Estrella only flirts
with the real drug dealers.
The ones who can maybe get her out of here.
Seems like that's where everybody wants to go.

Out of here. Even the drug dealers
are only dealing 'til they can make enough
money to bounce.

In the meantime, Estrella
wears their gold chain
    and takes a Polaroid with it.

A glimmering decapitated Jesus
dances around her neck.
Estrella got all the girls on the block heated.

Who does Estrella think she is?

Estrella thinks she is everything
    Mami wanted to be.
Estrella thinks she is nothing
    like Mami wanted her to be.

Estrella might look like burning afternoon
but inside she will always be winter.

PIRAGÜERO VS. THE LIMBER LADY

Everybody knows
who el piragüero is
'cause he is a man
you can't miss,
pushing around a carrito
that looks like he figured out
a way to jack the rainbow,
use it as an umbrella,
paint his icee cart with it &
pour it over a pyramid
of shaved ice to sell back to you.
I know that sounds real impressive.
But the real talent here
lives mad quietly on the third floor
of the most dangerous
building on the block.
A Puerto Rican flag on the window
lets you know that the limber lady
is open for business & all
you have to do is yell &
a bucket tied to a rope

travels out the window carefully
avoiding crashing into the
duct-taped second floor window
where the bucket has been
previously snatched from
bored-ass kids who find it
funny to see us wait for something
that will never arrive. Anyway,
if it makes it past the second
floor the bucket still has to make it
over the yellow bodega awning
until it gets to me swinging
back & forth like Mami does
when she's at the Check Cashing
spot waiting to be paid & so
I pay the bucket & watch it
float back up like Mami floats
when she's sure she can
pay the rent this month, up, up, up
it goes to get my limber
avoiding the same traps
that could still kill it on the way up.

SUMMER LUNCHES

The teachers say you have the power to choose
where your life is headed.

I think about that as my life heads toward
the long-ass summer lunches line.

When does that power kick in?
Maybe it's activated by a specific food

like how spinach moves through Popeye's stomach
and arms and suddenly he got super strength.

My styrofoam lunch plate don't got no spinach
but maybe in the hood the power lies

in peanut butter and jelly sandwiches.
I finish my sandwich and wait
for my strength to kick in.

My stomach rumbles but not in a powerful way.
Maybe I didn't eat enough.

I wait on the line for seconds.

NEW WORDS/AFFECTION/
A FEELING OF LIKING AND CARING FOR SOMEONE OR SOMETHING

The park and Mami have similar names.

Both heavy on the tongue.

The kind of name that's mad long for no reason.

This small connection to Mami makes me feel

like I could be the park's daughter too.

Like it could make up for Mami's cold ways.

On the days Mami refuses to hug me,

my body melts into the heat from an aluminum slide.

I join the park's summer youth table hockey tournaments

just to see if I am better at winning something

other than Mami's affection.

Even if I don't win,

for a moment,

I am good at existing.

I am celebrated for trying.

YELLOW TAPE

Yellow tape usually means
something wild happened on the block.

Someone died again or there was an accident
and we need to find a way around it.

The yellow tape usually goes away
after a few hours so we can sit with the illusion

that everything is safe on the block again.
Estrella and I look out the window at the yellow tape

that decorates the entrance to our block.
From our third-floor window it almost looks like a bow.

The cops are asking anyone who tries to cross
the tape for ID like the employees

at the Toy Drive do right before
they give you your present.

I look for the dark truth of an accident
or a dead body but the block

is a calm bright gift waiting to be claimed.
That's mad weird since

we've never been anyone's prize.

HOW WE GOT OUR NAMES
JEFFERSON STREET

Since the block is on lockdown
    and everyone had to show ID in order
to cross the police tape
that means G has to meet his clients
    one block over on the block named after the dude
who said all men are created equal

    & I wonder if he had any of us in mind
when he wrote that.

MY LIFE AS A SALSA SONG
PERIÓDICO DE AYER

Today I found out the library has old newspapers.
I disagree with Héctor Lavoe
that yesterday's newspapers have no value.
I want to read all of them.
History in school is mad boring.
But history in the newspapers
doesn't feel like history at all.
It feels like I'm eavesdropping
on everything that happened yesterday
so that I'm prepared for what may happen tomorrow.

THE NEWS ARTICLE IS ABOUT
HOW HOPELESS WE ARE

NEW YORK TIMES,
OCTOBER 6, 1993

Nobody talks much about Bushwick. It's just a tired, old, poverty-racked neighborhood in Brooklyn where adults without jobs move listlessly from one boring day to the next, and the police have to close off streets to slow the high-energy encroachment of youthful drug dealers, and the children, of whom there are many, find it difficult to dream because their days and their nights are so often disturbed by the sound of gunfire.

The kids in Bushwick grow up knowing that life is a crap-shoot, which means you may not grow up at all. The walls of many buildings are covered with huge and disturbing murals—elaborate graffiti memorials to friends and play-mates who died from a bullet to the head, a knife in the heart, and so on.

IF THE NEWS ARTICLE WAS ABOUT POLICE BRUTALITY

███████████████████████ *Bushwick. It's* ████████████
███████████████████████████████████ *where* ████████
██

████████████ *police have* ██████████████ *slowed the*
high-energy ███████████ *youthful* ███████████████
████ *children, of whom there are many, who find it difficult*
to dream because their days and their ███████████████
████████████████████████

██
██
██
████████████████████████████████████ *playmates*
died from a bullet ██████████████████████ *and*
so on.

IF THE NEWS ARTICLE WAS ABOUT HOW HOPEFUL WE ARE

████████████████████████████████████

████████████████████████████████████

████████████████████████████████████

████████████████████████████████████

████████████████████████████████████

████████████████████████████████████

████████████████████████████████████

██████████████████████████

The kids in Bushwick grow up. ██████████

████████████████████████████████████

████████████████████████████████████

████████████████████████████████████

████████████████████████████████████

████████████████████

THE BLOCK IS HOT

The Devil
used to be an angel named Lucifer.

According to the Bible
him and a whole bunch of his angel homies

tried to take over God's neighborhood
and a turf war broke out.

God won and as the winner
he got to keep the entire heaven with all the dope clouds

and the harps and the gold streets and shit.
As the loser, the Devil got kicked out.

Thrown into the hottest place God had created
just in case some shit like this ever went down.

Estrella is now in charge of warning Jesus
when there are undercover cops on the block.

If this were a biblical war
the cops and the corner boys would shoot

jabs at each other over who was Lucifer
but everybody would agree

that this neighborhood is hot as hell.

VOICES

Mami is acting weird. At night she calls me
and whispers: *Sarai, they are here again.*

I hear some voices outside but it's the summer
& warm weather is when Bushwick is most alive.

I tell her to get some sleep.
I promise they'll be gone in the morning.

WE RAN OUT OF TOOTHPASTE

It's Sunday & Mami says the Devil is using me.
She whispers a curse or prayer under her breath

as she flattens our church clothes on the bed.
The iron vapors its own praise toward heaven.

Estrella & I joke about our naked bodies
while we wait to be beautiful enough to matter.

We walk away slowly
to brush our teeth & whisper fight

over who's going to tell Mami
we ran out of toothpaste.

Tomorrow is Mami's face-to-face appointment
with the welfare office

& she needs her teeth clean as a lie.

BACK AT THE WELFARE OFFICE

Any other day no matter how tired I am
Mami reminds me that my legs work
fine, but today we are taking the bus.

If we late, we have to come back
another day and that's a waste
of a token that we could have exchanged
at the bodega for cash.

Mami smiles at every person
who looks important, like she is trying
to convince them she is no trouble.
I hope we get the Latina.

Mami thinks having a Latina caseworker
automatically works in her favor.
If we don't get a Latina, Mami will pretend
she doesn't understand English.

Sometimes this works
& we get assigned a Latina.
But other times I end up having to translate
about how poor and fatherless we are.

On the welfare line, my feet blister
& weep onto the floor.
Estrella & I are bored so we run
around the zigzag of slouched bodies
dripping with sweat and hope.

Mami has already used her voice
too many times today to waste it
on anything other than prayer,
but her angry whisper is sometimes enough
of a clamor to make us freeze
like statues deserving of worship.

TALK PROPER

Mami is hype they assigned her somebody
with a Spanish last name

who then starts to talk
to Mami in English.

She gives us questions
to ask Mami

& I guess we ain't translating them
the right way

'cuz the caseworker tells us we should practice
speaking proper so we can get *good jobs*.

So people *take us seriously.*
Speaking proper will get us places.

Like working at the welfare office
helping our own people, like she is.

She was once just like us.
Now she is somebody.

Speaking proper will help us belong
somewhere that has never made us feel welcome

even with our mouths closed.

HOW WE TALK

Estrella & I
are so alive,

our mouths
throw their own house party.

It's why we can't stay still
when we talk.

This isn't body language.
It's how we get free.

HOW MAMI TALKS TO PEOPLE WITH POWER

Mami speaks
differently to
the case
worker.

Softer—a voice
commonly used
around dead things.

Like a woman
attending her own
funeral.

GOOD JOBS

We should have seen it coming
with how quiet Mami got after the caseworker
let out a frustrated *Shhhh* as Estrella & me joked.
Mami raises her hand in the air like praise
and swings it down on us like a rebuke.
Estrella & I are so stunned that we don't even cry.
Mami never hits us in public.
The caseworker says she is a mandated reporter
& has to call the Bureau of Child Welfare Services.
Mami asks if BCW is gonna
take us away and I don't know if she wants the answer
to be yes or no. Sometimes I think she wishes
we were never born, but if we were never born
what would she do with all of her anger?
There are rules about hitting your kids in public.
It's not polite to make other people witness that shit too.
There are bathrooms and such she could have taken us to.
But now Mami put the caseworker
in an uncomfortable position.
She can lose her job if she doesn't report it.
The caseworker says:
It's not personal you know?
She just has a job to do.

BCW FROM A TO Z

And so just that fast
Bureau of
Child Welfare Services came to the apartment today
Dressed like undercover cops
Except they smiled and were so kind we almost
Forgot they were here to take us away but we ain't
Going nowhere 'cause we know what to say and how to say
Hello in a way that feels
Inviting like we don't got nothing to hide
Just in case they think they
Know how love works in this house
Love is a word we don't say to each other
Mami don't feel like she needs to say that
No one feels like they need to say that
Out loud anyway & for a while no one says anything at all
Probably because everyone is waiting for a
Question
Really everyone is measuring the
Silence in the way we measure
Time as in how long do we have
Until someone stops smiling and starts being
Vicious and then it happens Mami signs by the X

With her own
X which gives the nice people permission as in
Yes go right ahead and ask Estrella & me to un-
Zip to check for bruises

but all they manage to find are the spots that make us laugh.

NEW WORDS/ADDICTION/
THE REPEATED INVOLVEMENT WITH A SUBSTANCE OR ACTIVITY DESPITE THE SUBSTANTIAL HARM IT NOW CAUSES

Mami's been real calm since the BCW visit.
They closed the case since Estrella & I

didn't rat her out & it looks like our faith
in Mami has worked out.

Estrella & I haven't been punished
in weeks.

Tonight during prayer service
Mami clawed her hands toward heaven

like she was tryna scratch through a portal
or like she was offering up her demons in exchange

for children who weren't so hungry all the time.
The Holy Spirit pulled her body across the floor

to join a cemetery of sinners on the blood-fuzz carpet.
All these bodies, dying to live again.

I understand how you can become addicted to small
deaths
like the ones the Holy Spirit gifts you.

For a few minutes
you don't have to be responsible

for misusing your hands
on your children.

For a few minutes
all you have to hold is the floor.

BELL ATLANTIC IS BRINGING US TOGETHER

Mami's mother is Bori Wela.
She lives in Aguadilla, Puerto Rico.

Mami talks to Bori Wela every day now
that Bell Atlantic has a program

that helps people on welfare get a landline.
She hands me the phone & commands:

Ven, dile hello.

I'm not excited to talk to a woman I have never met
in a language I struggle with.

Unlike with Brooklyn Wela,
when Bori Wela talks to me in Spanish,

I answer in English.

        This way whenever we don't understand
each other
we both hum
& let the silence
fill us with wonder.

SILENT TREATMENT

Mami talks to Bori Wela the way she wishes I spoke to her.
Honestly & in Spanish. Mami and Bori Wela talk every day.

Sometimes Mami is so mad at me or life or something
that she doesn't talk to me at all,
but she still makes me talk to Bori Wela.

She thinks it's extra punishment
to have Bori Wela yell at me
for not helping out around the house
or causing Mami stress by existing.

I kinda look forward to how Bori Wela
breaks the silence between us.

Even if Mami goes back to a quiet anger, for a moment
she has to call my name

and I have to respond.

THIS IS YOUR BRAIN ON DRUGS

There is a commercial
that is supposed to stop me
from wanting to do drugs.
It involves a girl smashing
an egg with a frying pan.
Or a man frying an egg
to symbolize what our brains
look like when they are high.
The egg sizzles & pops.
We ran out of eggs two weeks ago.
I wonder what the brain
looks like when it's hungry.

HOW WE GOT OUR NAMES
CRACKING UP

Estrella & my favorite thing
to do is laugh together.

We laugh at everything.
Even shit that we not supposed to laugh at.

Like at dopeheads, any dopehead
who leans all the way over,

almost touching their toes
and never falling down.

We know it's not right to laugh
at someone else's addiction

but everybody is addicted to something
and laughing is our own habit to kick.

We crack up because everybody else
is tryna crack down. Crack down on drugs,

crack down on guns, crack down on graffiti
& all we can do is laugh and laugh until

our mouth becomes a weapon
that shoots joy into the air

hoping it lands on someone
on the way back down.

FALL DOWN SEVEN TIMES

In church on Sunday, the pastor prays for me.
He leans his palm heavy against my forehead.

I push forward but he yells
¡Fuera! so loud I jumped back

and suddenly my body is flying
backward toward the ground.

Later, Mami says I fell 'cuz the demons left
my body and made me lighter.

Estrella says I fell 'cause they multiplied
and made me heavier.

An hermana throws a blanket over my legs
to keep my dignity intact or to keep the men from sinning.

Every time someone faints the people praise louder.
It's a celebration to fall down and get back up.

I can hear and feel everything
but I keep my eyes closed

because I want my own small death.
I want to dream & wake up to a new reality

where even our demons are worthy of a loving God.

Where even they get to have a home
they don't have to leave.

GET UP EIGHT

Today I made a promise
never to laugh

at a leaning dopehead.
I know the strength

it takes to balance
all of your demons like that.

REHEARSAL

The man who plays the piano looks at me sometimes.
& I know that look.

It's the same look most men have when they look at me.
They want me to know that I am beautiful

as if only their acknowledgment can make it true.
Piano Man grazes my hand at drum lessons.

He touches me
as if I were a musical instrument too.

MY BODY

I didn't even start noticing my body
until the men did. Estrella says I'm lucky

'cuz men only notice the pretty girls.
If I was ugly I would be ignored

so I practice being ugly.
I borrow Mami's loose ugly, flowery skirts

but the men buzz around me and my ugly flowery skirt
like they tryna pollinate me or something.

TAG

After church Estrella and I act like kids
in the church parking lot.

There's a girl in church named Nini
who never says anything.

I wouldn't have noticed her
if I didn't understand how loud silence can be.

So I invite her to play tag with Estrella & me.
She accepts & we stash our *too big for this game*

bodies in between the parked cars and dodge
sudden death by way of the moving church van.

Hermana Santiago rolls down the van window
and screams at Nini to get in the van.

She yells that Mami should discipline us more.
It's in the Bible!

I can tell Mami is pissed off
by the way her eyes string themselves together

like she does when she's reading the Bible
with no glasses.

She burns her eyes through us
like she's trying to start a fire.

At home, Mami beats us like she hopes Hermana
Santiago can feel it.

Thank God for tag.

Estrella & I run from Mami
who is currently it.

THE MAGIC CHURCH BUS

On the nights Mami is in a good mood,
she lets the church van drive us home.

In the church van, people are allowed to laugh,
wonder and ask questions about each other's families

or gossip about whoever
didn't make it to church that day.

Mami brags about Raffy and how close she is
to getting him to convert.

A new soul for Christ is another
diamond on the crown Hermana Santiago reminds us.

The bochinche on the bus is always a good reminder
that Christians are human too.

In the church van, the adults
enjoy their humanity

more than they enjoy their God.
& I enjoy sitting next to Church Boy,

the bus driver's son.

THEY HAVE CABLE

Today we are visiting Nini from church.
Mami is trying to befriend Nini's mom,

Hermana Santiago,
I guess to prove to her she's not a bad mother after all.

I'm happy Mami finally has a sort-of friend
because it makes her normal like other moms

who have company over
and make fun of their kids

while drinking Pilón and eating galletitas
from the big green can.

Mami says that friends are like a dollar in your pocket.
I don't know if this means friendships are cheap

or that she's broke,
but today Mami must have a dollar.

Nini lives up the block from us
in a three-bedroom apartment

with Hermana Santiago and five of her siblings.
She's the only girl.

The boys are cursing and jumping off the couches
onto a yellow foam mattress when we arrive.

Nini yells at them to stop being such stupid idiots
before she slaps them.

They dare her to. Nini's mom flings her chancla
across the room as a warning.

Nini catches the warning across her cheek and cries
like she wants someone to hear her.

Mami says maybe we came at a bad time
and that we should go but they have food and cable,

so I walk over to Nini and give her a hug,
which is the only thing that's missing.

FOR ALL HAVE SINNED AND COME SHORT OF THE GLORY OF GOD

This is the Bible verse Hermana Santiago quotes

when I confess how guilty I felt
for laughing at the crackheads.

It's God's way of saying everyone makes mistakes,
she explains.

Is doing drugs a mistake?

Hermana Santiago says it is.

But what about the people who sell drugs?
Whose mistake is bigger?

Hermana Santiago gets real quiet
like she's listening for God to give her an answer.

Suddenly, she starts wilding out
and tells me that we are in no position to judge anyone,

user or dealer. It would do us real good
to look in the mirror

and see where we have fallen short
before we try to tower over anyone else

with our righteous attitudes.
I don't know who she's talking to

but suddenly it doesn't feel like it's to me.
It reminds me of when I practice reciting

all my good disses
in the mirror in case I ever get into a fight

where I might need to use them.

NEW WORDS/GLAMOUR/
AN ATTRACTIVE OR EXCITING QUALITY THAT MAKES CERTAIN PEOPLE OR THINGS SEEM APPEALING

This never happens but
today Mami wore pants

& marched mad
pissed off to the welfare office

to tell her caseworker
that she wasn't shit

for decreasing
her food stamps.

Never mess with a woman
dressed in the glamour of

her children's hunger.

FIRST JOBS

Lala got her first job working summer youth.
We celebrate her being one step closer to

making it outta here.
When you gonna get a job? Lala asks.

I been looking.
I lie.

The truth is my job is to help Mami keep track
of her appointments.

I never really asked Mami why she can't write
her own appointments down on the calendar

but it doesn't matter
'cause I like my job.

It has perks, like I get to ask questions
without being yelled at and I get to request new Bic pens

and keep some for myself
and because Mami has to make sure

that I get everything right
she has to speak so slowly

and so softly that I almost feel as important
as the case managers at the welfare office.

I wonder if they love their job as much as I do.
I wonder if they appreciate Mami's patience

with their questions.
I wonder if they miss her when she's gone.

QUESTION FOR THE BIC PEN I USE TO WRITE DOWN MAMI'S APPOINTMENTS ON THE CALENDAR

What are the stories you would rather tell?

TODAY IN BIBLE STUDY

Today's lesson is on the Tower of Babel.
It's the story of why we have so many languages
in the world. What had happened was the people
tried to get all slick and build a tower tall enough
to reach heaven and get to God.

I don't know why they were tryna get to God.
The Bible has a habit of leaving out a lot of detail
important to the story. Maybe he wasn't listening
or some shit and they felt like they had to go

regulate. Like when Mami calls the welfare office
about them messing up the amount she's supposed to get
and they don't answer the phone so she has to go in
person so they know she means business.

Anyway. Rumor has it they built a tower
so tall that they could almost taste the clouds.
Estrella & I crack up at the thought
of God being so childish and laughing
at how they thought they were smarter

than him and then waiting for the right moment
just as the people were starting to feel confident
in their unity, and with one flick of his wrist
or however it is that God makes things happen,
he made it so that they didn't understand each other;

and just like that we got the gift
of miscommunication all because God
was mad that for a moment
we were almost on the same level as him.

NEEDLES

Tone uses heroin. Sometimes we find needles in the bathroom or kitchen. They lie on the floor lonely, having served their purpose. Tone gets mad at Mami when she sweeps them up. *Those were clean needles I got from my friend!* he yells. Mami says she can get him real clean needles from her diabetes doctor. Mami sends me to la farmacia. I don't wanna go. *You're gonna help him get high?* I complain. Estrella tells me I don't get it. If Tone doesn't get new needles he can get sick. If Tone gets sick he can die. If Tone dies we are homeless again. I shut up and run to fill the script.

NEW WORDS/SCOFF/
TO LAUGH AND TALK ABOUT A PERSON OR IDEA IN A WAY THAT SHOWS THAT YOU THINK THEY ARE STUPID OR SILLY

Mami is seeing things again.
The oil drips from the walls;

she swipes the grease
onto her hands and tells me:

Mira, estoy ungida.
Look, I am anointed.

She rocks back & forth during prayer.
Mami says she is not crazy.

Just recovering from the neighbors' witchcraft.
She suspects someone has a voodoo doll

modeled after her to keep her sick.

The doctor Mami went to see called it schizophrenia.
Mami scoffs at this diagnosis.

Mami calls it *los nervios*.
An epidemic only Puerto Rican women suffer from.

Something only women with pins
in their body would understand.

NEW WORDS/EVALUATION/
A SYSTEMATIC DETERMINATION OF A SUBJECT'S MERIT, WORTH AND SIGNIFICANCE

Mami finally got approved for Social Security Income.
It's a check you get for being sick

and not being able to work.
Mami doesn't really talk about her illness much.

Papi says from what he can see
nothing is wrong with her

& calls her lazy for not trying harder to find a job.
SSI is different from welfare but it's money

we have to wait for regardless.
Mami thinks since Estrella has been acting strange

she can qualify for SSI too.
She makes an appointment to get her evaluated.

Estrella overheard Mami telling Raffy
that with an extra $500 a month

we can afford to buy more food.
Estrella thinks it's foul for Mami

to be fake worried about her for a check.
She says if Mami makes her go to the psychiatrist

she's gonna act crazy on purpose.

Maybe she can make extra money
from being an actress on Broadway.

I think Estrella would look fly on a stage.
She laughs and twirls, in love with her mad idea.

Come on, she says.
Let's practice what crazy looks like for Broadway!

Estrella imitates Mami when she's in a rage.
I decide to be Mami at her quietest.

MEDICAID

At the therapist's office, Estrella and I watch cartoons and giggle our thirst away. It's the end of the month and laughter sits in the back of our throats like cool water. The receptionist asks for our insurance and it's my turn to bring Mami her purse. A woman standing next to Mami fans through her credit cards and decides on one to pay for her visit. She mutters something to the receptionist about perfectly healthy people on welfare living off of her taxes. I give Mami our Medicaid card. White like good milk. Estrella says she should punch the lady in the mouth. I laugh and tell her to save her anger for the therapist.

LIVING THE DREAM

I had a dream where I write myself a new life
in a new town that believes in me
& I buy Mami a house she doesn't deserve.

In Bushwick, the only dream is finding the nail salon
with the cheapest acrylic tips & the only future
is the rare occasion Mami smiles like she found hope

or some money to take the bus downtown
so the therapist can sign a paper that says
that Estrella and I can't focus so we need

extra time on tests,
when really we're just alive and tired
of questions that don't ever answer our hunger,

distracted by the strange way
we're being given attention,
like we matter and don't at the same time

in an office whose doors lock and has air
that smells like it's never had roaches
so how could the therapist possibly see us

at our calmest when we got feet
that have never known to trust that the floor
won't spill the fury of a thousand rats.

MY LIFE AS A SALSA SONG
LA CURA

After the visit we get a free MetroCard if we sign out
with our Medicaid #. Knowing how we are getting back
home is the only good thing about seeing the therapist.
It's the least they can do after not believing us when
we said everything hurt but we couldn't really explain
where or how because what we mean is we have all this
pain and nowhere left to put it so sometimes it travels
our bodies and other times we have to let it loose if
someone stares at us long enough to see how scared
we really are even of our own brilliance. Estrella and I
want to be heard more than we want the medicine but
it's a quick visit 'cause the waiting room is full of
people who need to be seen before the MetroCards
run out.

AFTER SCHOOL THE PIANO PLAYER FROM CHURCH IS WAITING FOR ME

I get in the car because I know him.
I get in the car because he is the pastor's best friend.
I get in the car because he promised to take me home.
I get in the car because this could be God
sending me a blessing.
I get in the car because I need to save my feet
for the walk to church later.

because someone cared enough
to pick me up from school.
because it makes me feel like the white girls
I see in the movies.

because I want my friends to see me matter.

He starts driving me home & the car door is locked.
The streets abandon their homes
& the car door is locked.

We stop on the block where people make sure
their car doors are locked.

I know something is wrong
'cause I am not home and the car door is locked.
He wants me to smile.
I have such a pretty smile.
I regret learning it in the mirror.

I want to scream
but God probably won't hear me
if the car door is locked.

SARAI SHOULD HAVE KNOWN BETTER

The pastor asks how old I am and guesses 17, 18.
Mami says 13 like she's ashamed she gave me her hips.
I remind her I turned 14 last year. The pastor says
what he would have said regardless of what age I was.
I should know better than to get into a car alone with
a man. The pastor is pissed off but I can't tell if it's at
the piano player or at the fact that our church might
not have a piano player soon. Mami asks if we should
involve the cops.

The pastor says God is the highest authority

                                    and we pray.

THE PIANO MAN HAS A FAMILY

They place me in front of the door so I can be the first thing he sees when he opens it. I guess this makes it easier for them to introduce the subject. Kind of like knowing what the TV show is going to be about before you watch it. This time I am in a novela I didn't sign up to be the star for.

A pregnant woman opens the door, she looks exhausted. She shushes two toddlers behind her who are screaming and racing each other across the apartment. I smile at her like this is an audition and I want her to invite me to the next round.

She looks confused and annoyed. She ushers Mami, the pastor and me in without asking any questions.
I feel like I won already. There are only four seats at the table she points to. Mami, the pastor, the Piano Man's wife & me. This is nice. I wish we had a table. Good families always have tables.
I run my fingers across the dark wood. I wonder where the Piano Man will sit.

MY LIFE AS A BIBLE STORY: LOT'S WIFE

The Piano Man's wife
is looking straight through him.

She doesn't move,
like a beautifully carved pregnant statue.

I think all women have that talent.
To make pain look like art.

In Bible study we learned
how Lot's wife turned to a pillar of salt

because she looked back
at a town God was destroying because of sin.

I think it's real hard to leave something you once loved
and not look back one more time.

That's exactly how Piano Man's wife is looking at him
like he is a burning city God is warning her to leave.

WHAT ESTRELLA KNOWS ABOUT JUSTICE

Nobody's gonna save us but us.
Nobody is gonna protect us but us.
I just want to forget it ever happened.
But Estrella says we can forget after
Corner Boy Jesus reminds Piano Man
that he fucked with the wrong one.

JESUS OUR LORD & SAVIOR

Ayo, Star! Jesus always calls Estrella's name in English
when he wants her to come downstairs.

Estrella runs out of the building & into his arms.
Like she runs downstairs when Papi honks the horn.

I can't hear much from our third-floor window
but I peep Jesus' white tank top
looking all tie-dyed red.

Estrella reaches for Jesus' bleeding knuckles
as he punches the air like you do
when you tell a good fight story.

Like you do
when you won the fight.

I run down the stairs
to thank Jesus for sacrificing himself for me

but by the time I get there
he's already gone.

WHAT LALA KNOWS ABOUT JUSTICE

Lala stopped by the stoop today.
It's been a while since we've spoken.

Summer youth has her wild busy.
Lala says I don't gotta talk about it if I don't want to.

Sometimes we don't and sometimes we do.
When we do, we crack jokes about Piano Man and his
wack-ass music.

Bet he won't be able to play for a while
after what Jesus did to him.

Is it wrong that I'm happy he's hurt? I lay down in Lala's lap.
I want to give my body a safe home.

Lala strokes my hair & laughs an irresponsible laugh.
I guess we'll find out on Judgment Day.

WHAT THE MEN KNOW
ABOUT JUSTICE

When Mami tells Papi about Piano Man
Papi is furious at me for getting into

a car with a man. He doesn't
understand how I could be such a pendeja.

At the bodega Papi warns me
that men are no good.

Papi says even though he doesn't own a gun
he has hands as good as bullets.

The bodeguero says he doesn't know
what he would do if he ever had a daughter.

Papi & the bodeguero go on and on
about how badly men treat women;

not them though.
But they've heard stories

you know?

MY LIFE AS A SALSA SONG
USTED ABUSÓ

I feel like I have a new body.
One that I put on to pass for human.

Inside
I am a monster.

Inside
I am angry

that I let someone steal me
from me.

Angry that I sang songs with him.
That I fixed my pitch to match the keys.

Angry that I loved the way
The piano carried my voice.

Angry that I let him guide my hands
over the drums.

Angry that I trusted a man
to take me home.

When home was just a few blocks away.
When home was my body, an already fully furnished room.

I should have changed the locks like Mami,
crossed my legs tighter.

But I let him in. I let him in
'cause I was scared.

I let him in 'cause they say if a thief
tries to take something from you

let him have it
unless you want to die.

What a fucked up option to have
when both choices take your breath away.

My real body has been looted.
My real body has been thrown away.

My real body wants to crawl out of
where a man's guilt has buried it

& find its way back to me.
I know it. My real body visits me

in my dreams & this time we walk home
together. This time we trust only our

feet & the next step
and the next step

& the next.

THE LAST TIME I CALL
THE CHATLINE

Today I tell the truth about who I am on the chatline.
The coiled cord stretches straight as I walk to the mirror.

I had forgotten what I looked like.
Today, I decide to remember.

Today I am Sarai.
14 going on 15 from Bushwick, Brooklyn.

I start describing my body.
A body that is mine, and will never be anyone else's.

NEW WORDS/STATISTIC/ A FACT OR PIECE OF DATA FROM A STUDY OF A LARGE COLLECTION OF NUMERICAL DATA

Nobody wants to admit it,
but everyone is scared of something.

Sometimes anger
is how we show we are afraid.

Mami's case workers are afraid
they'll miss a lunch break

when the office is packed with people
who haven't eaten either.

Mami is afraid one day they'll send her home
with no food stamps at all.

Papi is afraid
I'll grow up to hate him like Mami does.

Estrella is afraid
of being afraid.

Danny is afraid
we'll forget his snacks when we visit him.

Bori Wela is afraid
Mami will never come back to Puerto Rico.

Lala is afraid
if she doesn't work hard she won't make it.

The cops are afraid
one day we'll decide we won't need them.

G is afraid he'll never make enough money
to quit dealing.

I am afraid
none of what I am afraid of will matter.

TONY'S PIZZA

At Tony's Pizza, Estrella and I peep
some weird couple eating
a slice with a fork and a knife.
Everyone around here folds

their slice in half, maybe because it's faster
to eat and we are always in a hurry
to get somewhere even
if that somewhere is nowhere at all.

Or maybe folding it in half only
requires one hand
and keeps the other free
in case we need it to tell a story

or protect ourselves from something, anything.

The point is, I learn
a lot about that couple
just by how they eat.
I know they not from here

'cause they not in a rush
and look mad peaceful
using utensils on a pizza
like they found all of the calm
and sliced it for themselves.

NEW WORDS/RESENTMENT/
A FEELING OF ANGER BECAUSE YOU HAVE BEEN FORCED TO ACCEPT SOMETHING THAT YOU DO NOT LIKE

The newspapers said
they gonna start planting trees

on the block
Mami is worried

    this means
    they are gonna raise the rent.

    No one but us
    can understand

this anger.
How poor

you have to be
to resent trees.

WELO

died before I was born. A freak car accident in Puerto
Rico. Brooklyn Wela tells me the story as she lifts the
mattress to pull out the envelope where she keeps her
money. The medics said they had never seen something
so gruesome. Welo was so unrecognizable they had to
have a closed casket funeral. But Wela didn't need to
see his face to cry. She is almost crying now retelling
the story. I feel bad for asking about Welo. For being a
metiche. *You must have been so sad*, I say. She laughs a
laugh I haven't inherited yet. She said Welo was so evil
not even the Devil would take him. She wasn't crying
out of sadness. She was crying because she was free. I
promise myself one day I'll cry for that reason too.

THINGS WE DON'T TALK ABOUT
PUERTO RICAN HISTORY

At home there are no history lessons on Puerto Rico.
We don't sing the national anthem around the table.
We don't talk about being Puerto Rican.

We just live it. You know?

We just eat Puerto Rican
We just drink Puerto Rican
We just dance Puerto Rican
We just sing Puerto Rican
We just pray Puerto Rican
We just fight Puerto Rican
We just cry Puerto Rican
We just laugh Puerto Rican
We just dress Puerto Rican
We just suffer Puerto Rican

& we love Puerto Rican too.

THINGS WE DON'T TALK ABOUT
WHAT HAPPENED TO MAMI

Everybody has a story.
But Mami doesn't tell us hers.

Estrella & I take turns guessing
who Mami was before she was our mother.

A Russian spy!
A salsa dancer!
A drill sergeant!
Yo. That last one though!

Estrella and I laugh
& laugh as we make up
pasts for Mami
that might help us understand
her present.

CHURCH BOY

My whole body shivers when I see him.
I blame the Holy Spirit in case someone notices my shaking.

I feel so guilty trying to figure out what
kind of sin Church Boy falls under.

I don't have any adults to ask about my crush.
None of the women I know have husbands
unless you count Jesus.

All of the women I know are waiting for a man
who left and promised to come back.

Even though she is dating Raffy
Mami says she is una mujer sola

as if her loneliness
is her greatest accomplishment.

I don't understand it but sometimes I'm proud of her.
How brave to not need anything but hope.

PICKUP LINES

Church Boy says:

I must have been a notebook
in another lifetime.

The one God kept in his back pocket.
With instructions on how to build the world.

FIRST KISS

Our first kiss happens in the church van.
We hop on before everyone else does.

When our tongues first meet they dance
like the white people do in the movies,
awkward but sure of themselves.

When it's over
Church Boy looks at me
like he wants me to say something
special about him.

But this was never about him.

END OF SUMMER

We know it's the end of summer
when the usually crack-ridden park
hosts a festival and tents it with meaning.

I sneak in a swing
while Mami watches the performers
move their bodies

in ways she has forbidden herself to.
Her eyes look busy with questions

and it fascinates me to see her curious
about something other
than how to keep us alive.

I HATE MY NEW HIGH SCHOOL

I didn't get into the school for gifted kids.
I didn't get into any of the schools I applied to.
I'm stuck with my Zone School.

Lala got into a good school in the city.
She's on her way to making it and I'm so proud of her.

At my new high school
the teacher throws a Blue Emergency card at my desk.
Said it had the wrong address.
She came looking for me and the lady
who answered the door said I didn't live there.

I stared her right in her pretend caring face.
Why you tryna come to my house anyway?
Today, I decide to be braver than my mother.

Today, I am a troublemaker.
A malcriada. My father's hands. An angry bitch.
I give my mouth permission

to be as dangerous as my neighborhood.
She matches my energy. High school teachers
be acting like they want smoke.

She said maybe if I came to school the first week
she wouldn't have to go look for me.
I've been cutting class a lot to hang out with Church Boy.
My new best friend.

THE COOL WHITE ENGLISH TEACHER

Curses, lets us curse
doesn't yell, lets us yell

Wears Tommy Hilfiger
& knows the latest hip-hop joints

Asks us what we wanna learn about
tells us things we shouldn't know

Like how she'll get in trouble with the principal
if they know she is the cool white teacher

So if they come by for a classroom visit
we'll have to pretend that we're doing work

& she'll have to pretend that she's teaching
& of course she's teaching but she may

have to yell at us to be quiet and if we don't
she may have to call our parents right then & there

So if we want her to keep being
the cool white teacher we have to listen

when people are watching
just so they know she's down

just so they know
she's doing her job

STRANGER DANGER

In high school, we have to prove
that we are not what the news says about us.

Even if what the news says about us is good.
Like when that genius kid from the hood got skipped
a few grades

and his family had to tell everyone it's 'cause
he reads a lot 'cause he ain't have no TV

and not because he cheats a lot like they say
about people like us on TV.

The white teachers won't say it out loud
but they feel sorry for us.

I can tell by how nice they are.
No one is that nice just because.

They kneel down by our desks
sacrifice their good knees for us.

They get real close to our faces
just like the news reporters do.

Just like they do at the welfare office
when they want to know if Mami is lying

about where she keeps
Papi's abandon.

They demand we look at them in the eye
while they tell us they understand us.

Pero, I don't ever see them on the block
so I know that they don't.

NEW WORDS/INVESTMENTS/
SPEND MONEY NOW TO MAKE
MONEY LATER

The cool white teacher says today's lesson
is about making money.

Class Clown TJ says
Hey, how come we don't ever learn
about stocks and bonds and shit?

A chorus of *woooooord* and *yooooo* carry a
challenge straight under the cool white teacher's nose.

The cool white teacher says it's complicated
and that we wouldn't really understand.

Try us, I push.

I mean to say we know mad complicated shit
the cool white teacher wouldn't really understand.

The cool white teacher is cool
when she explains.

It's like when you buy something now
you think might be worth something later.

Class clown TJ screams
like he figured something out.

Oh! Like when I buy Jordans!
Them shits is worth mad bread, miss.

No. The cool white teacher isn't cool anymore.
You can't invest in sneakers.

But you can invest in real estate.
Let me give you a real life example.

The cool white teacher uses investment in a sentence.

My husband...
Oooooh! all the girls who want someone to love squeal.

Her cool white husband is a real estate agent
and says houses in Bushwick are cheap right now.

Buying houses when they don't cost much
is a good investment 'cuz they might

be worth more later.
TJ feels dumb now.

I know because he cracks jokes whenever he wants
to let the teachers know they lost his attention.

Okay then.
Ask your husband if he wanna invest in some weed!

The cool white teacher
doesn't laugh with us & TJ like she normally does.

Everything cool about her is gone.
Now she is just the white teacher.

You want to go to jail, TJ?
Lots of new jails are opening looking for kids like you.

& I think I learned something new today.
I think she means that jails are someone's investments

but I don't know if that means someone thinks
we're worth something or nothing at all.

CLASS CLOWN

I don't know why we get in trouble for laughing.
If they saw how much time we spent crying

they would be encouraging our laughter instead.
One day our laughter will be revered.

Our laughter will have its own holiday & parade.
Our laughter will be a mandatory course
of study in school.

Our laughter will be researched
& analyzed by scientists.

Religious organizations will call our laughter
a false prophet, fearing we found a new god
in our smile.

We'll blast our laughter out of car stereos
in the summer so loud that they'll want to feature it
in the opening ceremony of the Olympics.

Maybe our laughter will be the torch.

Maybe they'll want to make our laughter
the national anthem.

Our laughter will cure our bodies.
Our laughter will be hereditary.

Our laughter will be as full
as the Check Cashing on the first of the month.

Our laughter won't ever be hungry.
Our laughter won't ever be worried.

Our laughter will stay strapped.
Our laughter will split skulls.

Our laughter will dance
like it's never had sense.

Our laughter will sound
like it caught the Holy Spirit.

Our laughter will be so much
of a miracle that God will give it its own heaven.

Maybe one day our laughter
will be so valuable

That someone will want to steal it.
That they will try to bootleg it.

That they will attempt to sell it back to us
at a higher price.

That we will have to protect it.
That it will have to come with a warning.

We'll have to tell our children
                    laugh at your own risk

& they will.
they will.

& maybe they do.
maybe we do.

SECOND PERSON

In English class you learn how to write in second person
and it becomes your new favorite way to exist.

Suddenly you don't have to be present-day you.
You can be you in the past.

You can write about your life like you're observing it.
You can write like you're wiser now.

Removed from all of the stupidity of the first person.
You are your smarter twin or you are future you

who writes to you in the past
& advises her to make better choices.

You hope this is on the quiz.

AN ENGLISH QUIZ I ACE

The English quiz is on figurative language.
& I have to write a poem using literary devices.

I think of how yesterday's newspaper
said the police call my block *The Well*.
& I laughed 'cause there are no actual wells in the hood.
            We lucky we even got water. Ha!
They mean it as a metaphor—
a connection between
two unrelated images.

If I had to break down the metaphor:
The deep down water would be the drugs &
the police would be the bucket &
that would make the 83rd precinct
the thirstiest village.

TONE GOES MISSING

It's been three days since Tone last came home.
In Bushwick, everyone is bound to go missing.

It's almost a birthright to disappear one day
like your life has earned the trouble

of being searched for. The truth is we all dream
of disappearing somewhere someday.

Mami wants to disappear back to Puerto Rico.
Sometimes, I don't think she even wants us to come.

Disappearing has to happen alone
in order for it to matter.

In order for it to matter, people have to wonder
and worry about where you could be.

Knowing you matter is the best part
about disappearing.

The worst part is not being around
to hear just how much.

SQUATTERS

G knocks on the door and asks us for the rent.
What? G is the landlord?

Tone's not coming back.
They found him overdosed in the park.

G said he owns this building
& a few others on the block.

He said he copped them when they were abandoned
back in the day when nobody

wanted to live next to
Black American & Puerto Rican people.

This building is still abandoned.
I curse G out in my head.

I'm so angry.
G's been behind this shithole this whole time.

He thinks he can get away with it
'cause he brings us corned beef every fifteen days?

We can't even sleep without
worrying if we're gonna wake up to enjoy it!

G says he'll give us extra time if we need it.
Matter fact: The next two months is on him.

& suddenly G is a savior again.

HOW WE GOT OUR NAMES
RAID

When the roaches multiply too much,
So much that you can't comfortably ignore them,
it's time to kill them.

> The best time to spray the roaches
> is when they don't see it coming.
> Either at night when they feel the safest

> or the moment right before the sun rises
> and they're scurrying back to their hiding places.
> Raid works best when it's a surprise.

You shouldn't be in the house
when a Raid is about to go down.
Raid can't tell the difference

> between you and what it's trying to kill.

THE NEW YORK TIMES

At the bodega I pick up a copy of *The New York Times*.
I try to unravel the long pages easily
like I know what I am doing.

I hold it a few exaggerated inches from my eyes.
I squint at it, hold it up toward the light

then pull it back again toward my face.
I inspect the paper like I wanna know

if it has an expiration date or some shit.
Goldo knows I am trying

to sneak read today's article about the drug bust
in our apartment building
without having to pay the fifty cents for it.

That's not a toy!
All the adults use this phrase

when they want you
to take things seriously.

The New York Times is serious.
I fold it up like a slice from Tony's

& shove it under my arm.
Goldo yells that I am messing up the paper.

I want to buy this—I say in a tone
I imagine the cool white teacher's husband would use

when he talks about investing
in our neighborhood.

I'm gonna buy this!
So I can do whatever I want with it.

BELL ATLANTIC IS TEARING US APART

The phone bill is way too high lately
so today Mami rips the twisty cord

from the phone and shoves it into
her purse as she leaves the house.

This way Estrella can't spend hours being a puta
on the phone with her boyfriend Jesus.

After Mami leaves, Estrella digs an extra cord from her
bra & resurrects the phone by reattaching the artery.

Oooh,
I taunt.
If Mami finds out
she's gonna kill you.

Estrella laughs a threat my way.
I look for another business to mind.

I know it doesn't really matter
if Mami tries to kill Estrella.

Some part of Estrella has already died.

I can tell because people who are truly alive protect
themselves from danger.

277

LOSING MY VIRGINITY

Lately, I spend most of my days with Church Boy.
We cut class & explore the city together.

Today we raced up & down
the Broadway Junction Escalators.

& took the J train
to Kosciuszko street.

Church Boy and I take turns pronouncing it.
Cos-Key-Yas-Co. That sounds about right.

We walk down Broadway until we get to Dekalb Avenue
Where Church Boy lives. We sit on the fire escape

& I remember what Señor Maví told me about
Bushwick burning.

Hard to believe this all went up in flames once.

Church Boy doesn't hear me though

His hands are already up my skirt
Trying to start a different kind of fire.

MAMI THINKS I AM STILL A VIRGIN

It only happened once so maybe
I think I still am too.

ESTRELLA GOES MISSING

Maybe it's because they think
you ran away with the boy who looked like God.

Maybe it's because they think
you'll come back three days later like you are God.

Maybe they are expecting you to resurrect like this
again, like you have always been a dead girl

waiting for the moment to rise,
glory and miracle.

Maybe no one is searching for you
because you being gone

is not enough evidence
that you were indeed missing.

You so loud so the police are sure
we will find you. Crying wolf. Crying.

You so loud that when you are silent,
they point us in the direction of your echo and say, look

a cave in love with her own darkness.
You are not a girl worthy of a torch.

You girl with bonfire hair, do not get to be illuminated.
You do not get to smile for the sake of being happy.

You have a grin ready for a mugshot.
They say it's your mouth that keeps you captive.

You're a name too hard to pronounce,
must mean you're difficult too.

Must mean you're not worthy of a chorus
to sing you into prayer.

Must make you a melody
we forgot the words to, a quiet hum.

It is no wonder you are missing.

IF BEING BORICUA IN BUSHWICK IS A FEELING IT'S THE WORST KIND

Not worst like we wish we were anybody else.
Worst like we know we not supposed to be us.
Worst like I can't believe Mami traded in a singing
coquí for a roaring M train lullaby.
Worst like we gotta wait on line for everything
especially our humanity.
Worst like everybody in our hood is Puerto Rican
but ain't no Puerto Ricans in our history books!
Worst like is history tryna tell us we don't have stories,
or that we don't have stories worth telling?
Worst like we belong to a missing people or something.
Worst like we know our people not missing
'cause we find them every day.
Worst like if I was to go missing, would someone try
and find me?
Worst like, damn, I hope I never go missing.

Worst like what if I am missing right now?

ESTRELLA IS BACK

& everyone acts like she never left.

GOT A SECRET,
CAN YOU KEEP IT?

Our church is on the corner
of Morgan Avenue & Thames Street.

This is the part of Bushwick
where people come to sin

and sinners come to die.
The church is the only holy thing

on this block. Before church,
Estrella and I race to the corner and hide

from God between the abandoned factories.
Estrella has a secret

and she makes me swear not to tell anyone.
I run through every secret-keeping pledge

I learned from Lala
whenever she tells me about her crushes or

a girl she's about to fight at recess.
Estrella is kind of like my homegirl.

I think these pledges apply here.

Cross my heart and hope to die.

Nah. 'Cuz If I accidentally told somebody,
that's my whole life.

Pinky swear.
Damn, that would require actual physical contact.
We not that kind of family.

I settle on what seems like the safest option.
I zip my lips, and lock the end of my smile
with a twist of my wrist and throw away the key.

Estrella doesn't buy my imaginarily zipped lips.
You can still open your mouth, stupid.

I keep them closed anyway, point to my mouth and
shake a thumbs-up towards her to signal
that the zipper really works & she can tell me.

She rolls her eyes so far back that I almost think
she's checking heaven to see if God found us.

Whatever. I had sex for the first time.
With Jesus. That's where I stayed the last few days.

She leans against the brick wall
like it's the first thing to hold her all day.

I post up next to her,
feel my hand melting into hers.

In Bushwick it's hard to be soft
when everything is so hard.

I don't know what to say
so I keep my promise & say nothin' at all.

LOVE

Church Boy tells me he loves me.
This is the first time I've heard the phrase.

It doesn't sound like I imagined it would.
He says it like he wants something from me

but he must know I have nothing to give
so I allow it.

I pretend I am happy to hear it.
Maybe I am. I haven't decided yet.

I ask him to say it again.
This time so I can start getting used to it.

This time so I can mouth along with the words.
Practice how they feel if I ever said them to myself.

HOW WE GOT OUR NAMES
TAG

Church Boy has a black book and he wants me to tag it.
I don't have a tag name yet so he suggests Nena.

Choosing a tag is important. On the news the mayor
calls it vandalism and at home Mami calls it porquería.

If you paid enough attention to the streets you would
know vandalizers are actually called writers

and that porquería is actually an art form.
Tagging up is the stuff of legacy.

Corner Boy Jesus' tag name is G.O.D.
He says it stands for Get Out or Die.

That it has a double meaning:

> 1. A warning to outsiders.
> 2. A promise to himself.

Technically with the extra "o" the tag should have been
G.O.O.D.

but Jesus is a respected writer so it's disrespectful to
question his philosophy.

G.O.D. was tagged on almost every wall in Bushwick
like Jesus was tryna bomb his way into heaven or
something.

Just like that, Jesus had people talking.
A good tag will give you notoriety.

& it don't matter if publicity is bad.
If people hate you enough it can almost feel like they
love you.

HOW TO GO MISSING

One day the city

          started paying

cleanup crews

        to paint over

            all the tags.

I wonder what

        it feels like

to be so visible

        that people want

             to make you disappear.

SILENCE

Church Boy runs his fingers
all across my thighs

like they were a bad neighborhood
that he knew the shortcuts through.

I apologize for my stretch marks
because I want him to say

don't worry about it
or *you're still beautiful*

but he doesn't.
He says nothing

and nothing
is sometimes saying a lot.

HAPPILY EVER AFTER

Sarai.

It is the fall again and my name
drops off Estrella's tongue
like a leaf from a tree.

She tells me about her idea to move
to Chicago, Pennsylvania or Florida.
Lots of Puerto Ricans live there too.

I'm always surprised to hear about other places
Puerto Ricans live in
besides Puerto Rico.

How they all get there?
Why are so many of us here?

Like when Ms. Rivera told us
about Boricuas in The Bronx.

I wonder why Puerto Ricans
would ever want to leave the island?

Either way, in a few more years
with all the money Jesus is making dealing for G

we can leave.
Buy a house.

Can you imagine?
Estrella is lost in her imagination.

A house? With a backyard.
Maybe even a pool!

It'll be the American dream
if we add a dog.

But we'll need a Rottweiler or some shit.
You know, for protection.

I guess she means no matter where we go
we'll never really be safe.

Even when we make plans to leave Bushwick,
Bushwick will never leave us.

MAMI THREATENS TO SEND ESTRELLA TO PUERTO RICO

In Brooklyn, nothing belongs to us
not even our mouths.

Mami can't stand Estrella these days.
Mami said she's been acting different

since she started dating
Corner Boy Jesus.

Ay Mami. Chill.
You buggin'.
I come to Estrella's defense.

Mami doesn't appreciate how I
give my tongue a lazy comfort, a home.

I know you don't talk to your teachers like this in school
—which is to say

she doesn't feel white enough to be respected.

AGUADILLA

Damn, what will Estrella do in Puerto Rico
when she doesn't even speak Spanish?

What a way that would be for Mami to abandon her.
Drop her in the middle of Aguadilla

with her mouth steady stuck in Brooklyn.
Estrella is threatening to run away again.

I calm her down. *Mami couldn't go back to Puerto Rico
if she wanted to. La piña está agria.*

Mami owes too much of herself to Brooklyn to leave it.

BORI WELA IS DYING

& all Mami did today was stare at the phone
waiting for it to ring.
We found out from Mami's brother, who was as much
news to me as Bori Wela dying.
Mami never talks about her family in Puerto Rico.
It's like she left everyone behind.
It's like that was the first death she knew.

ESTRELLA GOES TO LIVE WITH PAPI

Mami is stressed since hearing the news of Bori Wela
& the fighting with Estrella has escalated.

¿Pues entonces? Mami opens the door.
What are you waiting for?

¡Vete!

Estrella is free to leave and Mami is free
to pretend she didn't just kick her out.

Estrella grabs her best clothes.
She leaves me the wack ones.

She isn't sad to leave.
Maybe Papi's new wife

can be her new mother.

I MISS ESTRELLA

I tell Church Boy I miss Estrella.
I have no one to laugh with now.

& now there's only one of us for Mami
to take out her frustrations on.

Church Boy says I can always talk to him.
& we kiss until I have forgotten Estrella, Mami, Bushwick.

For a brief moment I feel
like I understand Julie's addiction.

How easy it is to love something
for how well it can distract you from your pain.

WE'RE GOING TO PUERTO RICO

Mami's brother has offered to pay
for Mami's ticket to Puerto Rico
to visit Bori Wela in the hospital.
He bought a ticket for me too.

I feel sad I can't share this moment with Estrella
& I feel guilty for being excited about going to Puerto Rico.
I make a note to learn the word
for having so many feelings at once.

I think of Señor Maví and his carrito.
The Puerto Ricans dancing on Fifth Avenue.
He'll be happy to know
that I finally get to learn my history.
I finally get to go home.

RAFAEL HERNÁNDEZ AIRPORT

When the plane wheels hit the ground everybody claps
like they do during worship & I guess it makes sense

to praise the landing.
Each passenger putting their faith in the pilot

& the flight attendants.
& for 3 hours and 45 minutes

we are the closest to heaven we will ever be.
Oh, how dope to be part of a glorious congregation in
the sky!

A rapture of Boricuas rising
like we always knew we deserved to.

Like Stars.
Nah. Nah. Nah.

Like Angels.
Nah. Nah. Nah.

Like chosen ones celebrating
this going home.

This second coming.

A TALE OF TWO PUERTO RICANS

Mami's brother meets us at the airport.
He is tall and looks just like Mami but with a goatee.

I watch the other families greet each other
with long hugs and sometimes tears.

They talk Spanish fast, no silence to fill with wonder.
Mami's brother leans in to hug Mami.

She extends her hand instead.
I extend mine too so that she doesn't feel alone

in her decision.
Mami's brother grabs my hand

and says I can call him Tío Richie.
Tío Richie,

I repeat like I want those words to mean something.
Like I want to brag about him in New York.

I have an uncle who lives in Puerto Rico!
Maybe I'll write about him in a school essay

or somewhere permanent like that.
I finally feel like I have some direct connection

to this strange land. Like if Puerto Rico is his
then maybe it could be mine too.

& just when I start thinking
that I finally belong somewhere,

Tío Richie jokes that I grew up
to be quite the gringa.

Suddenly, I feel like I don't belong anywhere.
Or maybe I belong everywhere.

PUERTO RICAN HISTORY

In the car with Tío Richie I try to search for the history
Señor Maví was talking about.

I look for it as we drive past the trees,
the beaches, and the colorful houses.

Maybe our history is in how beautiful the land is.
Maybe our history is in the language.

Tío Richie plays salsa on the radio and taps his fingers
on the steering wheel.

His hands dance as if they were their own body.
Mami is stoic. Stoic means without emotion. I think.

I remember what Ms. Rivera said
about music being inside of us.

Maybe history is inside of Mami and I just can't see it.
Maybe it's always been there.

Dancing. Laughing.
Waiting to be embraced

like the people hugging each other
at the airport.

Puerto Rico doesn't have the answers I am looking for.
Just more questions.

THE HOUSES IN PUERTO RICO

are pink and blue and orange and green

Is this legal? I ask Tío.

In Brooklyn

coloring any wall is grounds to get you arrested.

In Aguadilla

you get to live inside of your own mural.

Suddenly graffiti makes sense to me

as something that belongs to us.

A rainbow that seeps out of us

like some extension of our blood.

WHAT HAPPENED TO MAMI

We park on a hill. The yellow house
at the top almost looks like a sunrise.

When we go inside
I find out Mami has a sister too.

Maravilla runs and crashes into Mami.
Mami wraps her hands around Maravilla

as if she's been saving them for her
this whole time.

I've never seen Mami cry out of happiness.
Mami has a father too. He doesn't greet her.

He walks into his room
and shuts the door.

I notice that Maravilla talks the same way Danny does.
She rocks back and forth with excitement.

I think of Danny and his Cheez Doodle smile.
Mami kisses Maravilla goodbye and quickly leaves
the house.

She tells Tío that she is ready to go see Bori Wela.
She yells ¡*Avanza!* to us from outside.

What's up with Mami? I ask Tío.
Tío says: *You're too young to understand.*

I respond
Try me.

HOW WE TALK

TRY ME

Try me means take a chance on me.
Try me means I dare you.
Try me means don't sleep on me.
Try me is a threat
and a promise
at the same damn time.

VISITING BORI WELA
IN THE HOSPITAL

Only two of us are allowed in the room.
Tío offers to go in with Mami but Mami grabs my hand

and drags me
inside instead.

Bori Wela's white hair blends in with her pillow.
Her skin is yellow like our walls in Brooklyn.

There are tubes in her nose.
A machine next to her beeps

sounds just like a beeper going off
except the number on the screen is a heartbeat.

Bori Wela looks like she is sleeping
but the doctor suggests we say something anyway.

Says she can hear us. Mami's hand wraps around Bori Wela
super careful not to disturb the IV.

Mami. Llegué. Tarde, pero llegué. Guao. Te pusiste vieja. Jaja.
Te traje a Sarai. Sarai, dile algo a tu abuela.

If we were in Brooklyn this would be the part
where Mami hands me the phone.

I feel terrible for all of the times I felt annoyed
to speak in Spanish.

One day, just like the phone,
this machine will stop ringing.

This is my last chance to fill the silence with wonder.
I grab Bori Wela's hand.

I don't know what else to say
except the obvious.

Hola Wela.
Aquí estamos.

Estamos aquí.
We're here.

I can feel Bori Wela's hand squeeze mine.
I imagine this is how her hand held the phone

whenever Mami called.

IN CASE OF EMERGENCY
LEARN PUERTO RICAN HISTORY

Tío Richie asks Mami if he can take la Gringuita
on a drive to San Juan.

By la Gringuita he means me
and laughs like he's a comedian.

I beg Mami to let me go.
She asks Tío Richie if his wife is coming.

Tío Richie says she's already in the car.
Mami reluctantly agrees. Reluctant is a new word.

It means she almost says no.
But she doesn't say yes either.

She just purses her lips
and uses them to point

to her purse. I run to the brown crocodile skin
purse and hand it to Mami.

She pulls out twenty dollars
& tells me to use it *en caso de emergencia.*

Tío Richie, do you know Puerto Rican history?
We're heading there right now, he says.

GETTING TO KNOW YOU
GETTING TO KNOW ALL
ABOUT YOU

It's a long-ass drive from Aguadilla to San Juan.
I imagine this is what it feels like for Ms. Rivera
and Papi to travel to Brooklyn from The Bronx.
Tío Richie's wife's is nice enough.
Her name is Consuelo
but there is nothing comforting about her.
She's definitely the opposite of that
on this car ride. Consuelo talks fast and often.
She's also way too affectionate for my taste.
She's riding shot gun and somehow her long-ass arms
manage to reach over to the back seat.
Touching my hair. Caressing my face. Tapping my knee.
She thinks I am *so beautiful.*
You look exactly like your mother when she was younger.
¡Igualita! ¿Verdad, Richie? An exact mirror!
She wants to know all about my life in Bushwick.
How's school? Do I like boys yet?
I got *so big!* She remembers
when I was born & now look at me!

Time flies! Man, how time flies.
How's the new apartment?
She says she knows how rough it must have been
to move around so much.
I can't answer one thing
before she's on to the next.
I don't even know this lady
and she could write a biography on
my life. She said Bori Wela would update her
on how us & Mami were doing in New York.
I may not know a lot about Puerto Rican history
but I know Puerto Ricans love bochinche.
Consuelo would make a good journalist,
or a terrible one.
Déjala hablar, Tío Richie scolds his wife.
He's sure I have questions before we head back.
Why did Mami leave Puerto Rico?
Suddenly nobody is talking fast.
Suddenly no one is talking at all.

TÍO RICHIE WANTS TO TALK PUERTO RICAN HISTORY

I can tell he's tryna avoid my question about Mami
But I'ma let him rock.

Let's seeeee. He stretches the "e" out real professor-like.
Where do I start?

He says he can start as far back as when the Spanish
displaced the original Native people out their home
Borikén.

Displaced? Is this what happens in Brooklyn
when the cool white teacher's husband
buys up our buildings?
I think to myself.

Or when Spain started transporting enslaved Africans
to the island & killing off the Natives.
Or when the rebellion against Spain
called el Grito De Lares occurred.
Or when slavery was finally abolished.
Or when the United States invaded Puerto Rico

Or when Puerto Ricans became U.S. citizens.
But not really, 'cause we can't vote for president, he laughs.

Or the Ponce Massacre
when police opened fire on peaceful protestors.

Damn, that sounds like Bushwick
after the Puerto Rican Day Parade!

I make this connection
out loud.

Tío Richie pauses, confused.
I take this opportunity to breathe. Deep.

Damn, Tío, you're like a whole-ass historian.
I think of Señor Maví & decide to test his knowledge.

Is it true that the flag was illegal to own?

Tío Richie laughs, then says:
Why do you think we wave it so hard?

I want to laugh too
but I am so angry & so afraid.

Angry I didn't know.
Angry there weren't books in the library about this.

Afraid I'll forget all of this history.
Afraid I'll remember.

DIASPORICAN BLUES

I didn't know any of this.
Tío tells me not to feel bad

that he didn't know either
till he went to college.

But I don't feel bad.
I am angry & I put the blame on Mami.

I tell Tío Richie
that I am so mad at Mami

for not telling me
how many Puerto Ricans fought

and are still fighting
for their independence

so that I could be the proud-ass Boricua
waving a flag

on 116th Street every year.
Tío Richie says

People who leave the island are part of the diáspora.
Diasporican, if you will.

Then Consuelo lives up to her name
& says the first comforting thing

I've heard all day. She says that
leaving the island is a hard decision.

and that ever since Mami
moved to New York

she's spent her life
just trying to survive the day.

& if you think about it, really think about it,
staying alive, well, that too is Puerto Rican history.

WHAT HAPPENED TO MAMI

Mami's father had lost his job
en la finca due to some new
government project that was
supposed to make life in Puerto Rico
easier for everyone but instead
left Mami's father trying to figure out
how they were going to survive.
Mami couldn't be bothered
with her father's problems
'cause she met Papi
and fell in love.

But Mami's father didn't approve
and would call Mami the same names
Mami calls Estrella when she's
angry. *Puta. Sucia. Callejera.*

Soon Mami was forbidden
from seeing Papi but she would
sneak away during school hours
to play hooky and see him anyway.
When Mami's father found out
he locked her in a room.

Damnnnn. Like Rapunzel?
Tío Richie says: *Who?*
I say *never mind*
& invite him to go on.

Tío Richie says he didn't see Mami for weeks.
Bori Wela fought & fought with Mami's father
until he agreed to let her out.

The next time Tío Richie saw Mami
she asked him to help her run away.

Away from her father.
Away from Puerto Rico.

But Tío Richie felt that all Mami had to do
was follow the rules like he did.

Tío Richie says he's not a man of regrets.
But he regrets doing nothing.

Doing nothing is sometimes
the worst thing you can do.

MAMI & PAPI'S LIFE AS A SALSA SONG
PERIÓDICO DE AYER

So Papi told Mami he couldn't be sure but he had heard
there were better opportunities in New York
for Puerto Ricans. They could be together &
live better than they did in Puerto Rico.
It was a win-win! He knew a guy who knew a guy
who knew a guy that could get him a job.
A good job. & just like that they bounced.
Since Mami couldn't write well
she'd clip photos of her new neighborhood
out of newspapers and mail them to Bori Wela.
It's as if Mami was the journalist of her own life
& her life in Puerto Rico was old news.

MY LIFE AS A SALSA SONG
TODO TIENE SU FINAL

Bori Wela passed away
as we boarded the plane
back to Brooklyn.

Mami declined Tío Richie's offer
to extend the plane tickets so that
we could stay for the funeral.

Life goes on
Mami said
wiping away tears.

How life went on
with Mami & Papi

after they left
Puerto Rico.

How life is going on
with Estrella & Jesus back in Brooklyn.

How life will go on
for Lala & Ms. Rivera.

I wonder how life went on
with Piano Man and his wife.

Mami, I plead. *Let's stay.*
Wela would have wanted that.

Staying won't bring her back.
You can't change what happened in the past

Mami says.
Maybe to herself. Maybe to me.

Todo tiene su final.
Nada dura para siempre.

BOCHINCHE

Back in Brooklyn
Estrella is pregnant.

No one knows what to do.
Papi came down all the way from The Bronx,

on a weekday
to greet us with the news!

He's storming through Brooklyn
looking for Jesus.

Mami is blaming Papi
for letting Estrella run wild.

Estrella is hype for the chance
at being a better mom than Mami.

IMAGINATION GONE WILD

Estrella is back living with us.
At least until the baby is born.
After that she has plans.

Jesus & her are leaving Bushwick.
She says Jesus has been working hard
to get everything the baby needs &
they found a cheaper apartment in The Bronx.

Estrella says the baby will have Jordans & a fancy crib
that converts into a toddler bed. I'm confused.
But you don't even have Jordans & we share a bed.

That's the point, Estrella says.
Her baby will have everything we never had.
I'm still confused. *How can we give what we don't have?*

You gotta think about it first, dummy.
Estrella says in order to get what we want
we gotta imagine it first.

She says it's like
window shopping
for your dreams.

I'm determined to prove I'm not dumb.
Imagination is not real though, duh.
It's as good as the fiction I read.

Estrella looks at me as if I said something brilliant.
Exactly dummy, now go write yourself a book.

PLAYING HOOKY

Instead of going back to school I meet Church Boy
under the elevated train by the cuchifrito spot
on Knickerbocker.

I miss the sound of the coquí but not more
than I missed the sound of the M train.

I tell Church Boy all about what happened to Mami
and about Puerto Rican history

and ask him if he thinks it's weird that they
don't teach us this in school.

Church Boy tells me that I'm talking too much
and kisses me until my heart flutters like

the M train is running right through it.

THE 411

My new job is to spy on Corner Boy Jesus for Estrella.
She wants to make sure he's not doing nothing
with nobody. Whatever that means.

Today, I report back that I peeped Jesus
give Hermana Santiago's daughter Nini mad money.

Yo. You think Nini running drugs for Jesus?
Like some kind of child drug ring?
Think about it? Who would suspect a child?
Oh! You know what's even better than a child drug ring?
Abuelas hustling smack! Yooo that's genius.
& also real messed up. You think G is in on this?

I want to gossip with Estrella.
I want to laugh and imagine ridiculous worlds.
But she's not in the mood.

Nini is Jesus' sister, stupid.
The money is for their mom to pay the bills.

& suddenly I know why
Hermana Santiago is so angry all the time
and also why they have cable.

ESTRELLA GIVES BIRTH

Noah is born on Halloween.
Just like Estrella.

She turned 18
and I know

the newspapers
say teen pregnancy

is a curse that plagues us
but today on her birthday

she declares God gave her
this baby as a birthday gift.

She named the baby Noah.
If I had to guess

she imagined
this exact moment

where she would
get to choose

a name that meant something
a name that changed everything.

Noah, conqueror of floods.
Noah, who made her an ark.

WHEN WE MAKE IT

We're supposed to wanna get outta here.
When we make it, that's what we're supposed to do—
leave.

That's the dream. Make it out the hood.
No one tells us where we're supposed to go though.

       So, I got questions about leaving.
   We are supposed to go live where?
& with who?

   & if we leave the hood doesn't that mean we gotta
   leave
   our friends,
   our family,
   our bodegas,
   our stoops and shit?

   Just like the Puerto Ricans who left the island
   to come
   to the Lower East Side, The Bronx, Bushwick,
   Chicago, Florida, Pennsylvania.

But, okay,
say we make it
    big enough,
    rich enough,
    bougie enough

    to take everybody with us—we give Goldo
    enough money to open a bodega
    in the new hood, oh and we give the boys on
    the corner
    new corners to dream on—then isn't that just
    replicating the same hood
    we just tried to leave?

    Why are we leaving if we can't take none of this
    shit with us?
    If we can't take no one with us?
    Isn't that just running away from everything that
    made us?

    Who taught us to be so afraid of ourselves
    that the dream is to find new places
    & new people to be afraid of us too?

HOW WE HONOR OUR DEAD

The newspapers said it's real sad to see a new mural
highlighting the death

of another corner hoodlum.
It wasn't just one of the corner boys. It was Jesus.

The article says the cop that killed him was afraid for
his life.
Everyone got questions about that except the news.

They got Jesus' picture in the black & white mugshot
plastered all over the front page.

Everyone is gathered around the mural telling stories.
Jesus was tryna turn his life around for Estrella and
the baby.

He was getting his G.E.D.
Estrella says he talked about being a social worker.

Hermana Santiago said when he was little
her son wanted to be a cop. Ironic.

Maybe to some people
it doesn't make sense

to talk about a dead person's dreams
after they are dead.

But we know how important it is to show all of who
a person is.
All of who they could have been.

I agree with the papers.
It is really sad to see a mural for Jesus.

But the newspapers also don't know shit.
The mural for Jesus is not meant to highlight his death.

It's meant to celebrate his life.
That's why we picked the biggest wall

and the dopest graffiti artists in the hood.
That's why we use the brightest colors

and asked Jesus' moms for the best picture
she got of him so we can always remember him like that.

In color.
That's why we light candles

and place them on the block
and airbrush *Rest in peace G.O.D.*

on T-shirts in the brightest neon letters.

Even if in life we live in the shadows,
in death we live in the light.

HOLY WALLS

At church, the pastor uses the sermon to teach us
a lesson. He says the murals glorify the victims of
the drug war as if it's some kind of trophy to have
your face on a wall. *¡Amén!* He says the neighborhood
shouldn't be a cemetery. *¡Alabanza!* It should be a
garden. We should plant the seeds of Christ, not bury
bodies. *¡Gloria! God should be on the wall, halleluyah!
Let's spray-paint the walls holy. ¡Alábalo que Él vive!* On
the way home *God should be on the wall!* replays like a
song on a loop.

I walk by Jesus' mural.
God should be on the wall!

& today he is.
& today he is.
Amen.

ESTRELLA IS NOT THE SAME

& I recognize this feeling.
We all inherit a sadness we don't know what to do with.

Some of us stuff it into our laughter.
Others in a suitcase to New York.

Other's cook with so much sadness
it's how we salt our food.

We all have plans to go somewhere that's better than here.
Wherever here is.

But we never plan to die.
No we never plan to die.

NEW WORDS/POSTPARTUM DEPRESSION
A FEELING OF DEEP SADNESS, ANXIETY, ETC., THAT A PERSON CAN FEEL AFTER GIVING BIRTH TO A CHILD

It's the middle of the night
and baby Noah won't stop crying

like babies do when they're hungry
or need their diaper changed
or just want to be held.

Estrella never gets to figure out which one it was
and we never get to figure out if the shrieks
are coming from Estrella or the baby.

We follow the sound
just in time to witness the kind of quiet that happens
when somebody finally gives up.

Estrella has a blanket pressed over the baby's face
as she rocks him back and forth while singing
something in between an alabanza and a lullaby.

¡Llama a la jara! You know it's serious when Mami suggests
involving the cops. Mami snatches baby Noah
from Estrella's arms.

Noah is okay.
Gracias a Dios Mami says.
Today she is God.

Estrella just cries.
She doesn't fight back or even notice her empty hands
still in the position of a mother rocking her child to sleep.

PSYCHOLOGICAL EVALUATION

The doctor asks Mami why Estrella broke.
She blames our neighborhood,
el Bloque, with all of the fast girls.

In her version of the story,
Estrella is a lonely race car,
engine on, running the streets
wasting gas on men
who will never love her.

The doctor asks Estrella why
she broke. She blames Mami and
her frostbitten fingers.
She explains that Mami is sick
and cold and never loved her.

In her version of the story
she is a lonely race car,
engine off, who knows that waiting
for someone to love you

will drive you crazy.

WE VISIT ESTRELLA AT WOODHULL HOSPITAL

It's good to see her
laughing.

Estrella jokes
that she comes from

a cracked rib
& that's why

she's in here.
I try to join in on the joke.

Word. If you're part of some
breakdown in God's design

why are we made to
believe everyone is created

in God's perfect image?
Maybe if we knew

early on that God
had crazy days too

we wouldn't be
so ashamed of our own.

Estrella scolds me.
God didn't have crazy days.
He had creative days.

All of us are different
because God is a motherfucking artist.

I think of Danny & Maravilla
being created in God's image.

Maybe this even applies to Mami.
God's perfect image, huh?

If God is creating self-portraits
then we are all just unique variations of God.

ESTRELLA WANTS ME TO KNOW

When she gets out of the hospital
she's going back to school.

Don't get it twisted.
She doesn't think she needs to prove to anyone

that she's smart or nothing.
Matter fact she already got mad skills

that could maybe
help her graduate faster.

She wants to prove to herself
that she can do it.

& I know what it's like
to want to be better than yourself.

So I start planning with Estrella.
I sit on her bed just like if it was our stoop.

BROOKLYN WELA ADOPTS THE BABY

Mami says: *Don't worry*
you'll get him back.

In a way that maybe she wishes
someone had told her about Danny.

Estrella says she's just glad he's safe.
She's just glad he's safe.

BIRTHDAYS ARE STILL THE WORST DAYS

This year my birthday came and went
& no one said a word but I'm still here.

The one thing I learned in Puerto Rico is
that there are worse things than being forgotten.

Like being deliberately erased.

ONE DAY CHURCH BOY
STARTS ACTING ALL FUNNY

like he's tired of hearing about my problems.
It's not even like
I'm asking him to solve them.

Boys can't even listen
without feeling
like it's too much work.

Then leave.
I say this in Mami's voice
So that I can believe that I mean it.

GAINING WEIGHT

Church Boy says
I am getting fat

but my size has never
been a problem for me.

I am shaped like the moon
& on Knickerbocker Ave.

men howl themselves
into a werewolf at the sight of me.

I AM PREGNANT

Mami knows about it first.
Says I am sleeping too much
& gaining weight real fast.
She buys a pregnancy test
at Duane Reade & asks me
to pee on it. I argue my case
against peeing on the stick
but she sounds like she
wants to forgive me.
For a moment I have a mother
& who wants to pass on that?

MIRROR

& so I've seen this before haven't I?
I am my mother's reflection.

I am my sister's shadow.
I am everyone I tried not to be.

I am them.

                                        & they are me.

I TELL ESTRELLA I AM PREGNANT

as she is preparing Tone's old room
for baby Noah's return.

She is the happiest I've ever seen her
& I don't want to upset her.

I tell her that I'm worried
I'll be a bad mother like Mami.

Or that I'll have terrible postpartum like she did.
Estrella is not upset at all. She reminds me

that I am my own person
on my own journey.

I am my own person
on my own journey.

UNDERSTANDING TRINITY

The mother is not the daughter.

The daughter is not the spirit.

The spirit is not the mother.

They are all God together.

They are all God apart.

NEW WORDS/DETONATE/
TO EXPLODE WITH SUDDEN VIOLENCE

Church Boy said he's not ready to be a father.
I gotta approach this wisely.

If I curse him out, I may lose him.
If I stay quiet, I may lose myself.

Mami taught me how to scream
with my mouth closed.

I get my loud from her.
My *who you think you talking to* from her.

Even when she is quiet
there are explosions going off inside of her.

I detonate like her sometimes.
It scares me.

Mami taught me how lethal
a woman's mouth could be.

How it could cut someone sin cuchilla.
How to spit a knife straight through a heart.

How my mouth is an open wound.
A pocket that stores the weapon.

DISCIPLINA

The pastor sighs like he knew I was trouble

since Piano Man.

His wife smiles and holds my hand

while the pastor tells me how things will be

different. There's a section in the back of the church

for sinners. *Like hell?* I think.

People who fall from God's grace, his wife interrupts.

I'm not allowed to lead church service anymore.

I can only approach the pulpit when I am called to do so.

Or when you need prayer,

the pastor's wife interrupts again.

I am not allowed to play any instruments;

not the tambourine,

not the clave, not the güiro and not the drums.

You can still clap

and use your vocal instrument to praise the lord.

She's full of useless good news.

Who will play the drums? I ask.

Church Boy will, the pastor says.

Until they find a replacement.

Both of us have sinned

but only one of us fell short

from the glory of God.

BREAKING UP WITH CHURCH BOY

I told Church Boy I didn't need him.
Sometimes you gotta remind boys of that fact.

That you were somebody before them.
That you'll be somebody after.

I stood in front of him glowing
like I imagine Jesus did

after he resurrected
& before he bounced back to heaven.

Church Boy looked at me with all the doubt
Thomas had when Jesus showed up all radiant & shit.

I guess he thought I would die without him.
& maybe a part of me did.

But even Jesus knew that some deaths are necessary
to ascend into glory.

FIRST PRENATAL APPOINTMENT

Sarai, today you get to meet your baby.

Everything is happening in slow motion.

The doctor keeps talking

> but the last words he said replay in my head.

The baby.

> I'm gonna meet the baby.

I'm gonna have a baby.

I think that makes me someone's mother.

> No. Okay. Maybe not yet.

But it does make my body someone's home.

Body.
Home.
Mother.

Every word feels more dangerous than the next.

> Every word makes me want to learn a new one.

SONOGRAM

That's how I'll meet the baby.
A sonogram takes pictures of the baby

inside of my uterus.
Uterus.

I'm learning medical terminology for parts of my body
I never even knew I had.

It's kind of exciting to learn
new things about my body.

To understand yourself in a new way
means to love yourself in a new way

too.

BABY PICTURES

Dear Unborn Baby,

The doctor asks me
if I want him to print out a copy of your first picture.

Do people actually say no to this question?
I want a memory of this moment,
of the first time I see you.

I want to save it for
         when the school assignment
asks you to bring in a baby pic

& you show up with a black & white
picture of you in my belly.

        Make everybody laugh.
Go ahead, be the class clown.
& let the teacher call me complaining.

So I can laugh in her face too.
We can be a chorus of clowns in a circus.

        I want you to have everything I never had.
I want you to be everything I could never be.

But I don't say that to the doctor.
        I just say yes. I'd like a picture.

AT THE COUNSELOR'S OFFICE

Everyone has a job to do
and mine is to be the girl somebody saves.

I want another job.
The one where the girl saves herself, maybe.

But that doesn't help anybody get anywhere
and everybody wants to go somewhere.

The counselor wants to go home.
I can tell by the way she sighs

when I tell her I am pregnant
like I am a job she isn't getting paid overtime for.

I AM A DANGEROUSLY BAD EXAMPLE

The counselor is transferring me
        out to a school for pregnant girls.

She said it's a safer space for me.
        But didn't I die in some of the safest places?

& didn't the church ask me to forgive the man
who made my body a sad hymn?

& don't our stomachs growl while the news watches?

& isn't my hood where I learned to love
everything that hates me?

I smile at the counselor like she's doing me a favor.
Like Mami does at the caseworkers.

But there are no favors here.
Everyone is just doing their job.

& my job is to smile.
& my job is to not die.

FIRST DAY AT THE SCHOOL FOR PREGNANT GIRLS

I walk into the soundtrack
of new babies trying to convince their

mothers to miss first period.

The daycare makes me smile.
It also makes me sad.

It is a reminder that there is a school for mothers.
But there is no school for fathers.

MAMI SAID I'M A WOMAN NOW

& I gotta do woman things.
Like keep track of my own appointments.
& figure out how to buy my own bras.
She hands me my social security card,
birth certificate & immunization records
as if they were diplomas I earned.
Being a woman comes with paperwork
but none of those papers are instructions.

THERE IS NO ROOM IN THE BUDGET FOR BOOKS

At the School for Pregnant Girls
we read off loose sheets of paper
xeroxed from the teacher's only copy.

We don't really talk math unless
we are discussing how many weeks
we have left till birth.

The teachers keep us busy sewing quilts
for the babies' cribs.

I don't know how that's gonna help us
get into college.

They say this school is closing soon.
I wonder if it ever opened.

THE WRITING ASSIGNMENT IS TO IMAGINE FUTURE YOU WRITING TO PRESENT YOU

Shit. You're pregnant. Damn. You're not even 16 yet.
Shit. Stop crying. It's okay. You're okay. Stay in school.

I said stay in school. You shouldn't have let them kick you out.
You should have cursed at your guidance counselor.

Said something like *I'm pregnant, not stupid.*
It's okay. You're not stupid. Stop crying.

Yes, he's gone, but it's better that way.
It'll teach you about gravity and space

and boys who will love you
like a black hole

as if they can swallow you
without chewing.

Your stomach will start to globe soon
and you'll feel like the prettiest piece of earth.

It's time now. Look, no one will be here for you.
You know that. You're ready for that.

BABY SHOWER

I wish I would have known about the baby shower.
I would have gathered the energy to comb my hair.
Maybe even worn a nicer outfit.
I'm rocking Mami's T-shirt and an ankle-length skirt
which drapes over my pregnant body
like curtains attempting to hide the sun.
I look around the room for Mami . . . Papi . . .
Estrella can't come 'cause she's busy studying for her GED.
Maybe Lala will show up.
Nobody I love is here.
Nobody who loves me is here.
I don't even see Church Boy.
The church people say they love me
but my name is spelled wrong on the cake.

C-SECTION

The operating room is as cold as a Brooklyn winter.
I am alone & that makes it colder.

The nurse gives me an epidural.
She says it's to numb me.

Who am I if I don't feel pain?

I am worried
about giving birth.

I've gotten used to owning two heartbeats.
I don't want to be alone again.

Stop crying, Sarai. It's okay.
The nurse holds my hand.

You get to meet your baby soon.
Maybe I've been looking at it all wrong.

Maybe giving birth is different.
Maybe it's the most beautiful kind of abandon.

I GIVE BIRTH TO HOPE

I name the baby Hope because
Hope is a good name for a girl
who will have to grow up
believing in herself.

VISITING HOURS

Mami swings through and tells me she's proud of me.
I don't know what to do with her kindness but I decide

maybe I don't have to do anything but accept it.
Estrella switches places with Mami 'cause babies aren't

allowed on the floor. She's happy baby Noah has a cousin
to keep him busy while she tries to get her degree.

Kids are mad work. You'll see.

Papi comes through
with a salami, turkey and cheese sandwich

from the bodega but he forgot my tropical fantasy.

What you gonna do for a job?
Don't end up on welfare like your mother!

But I'm too busy scarfing down the hero
to appreciate his ridiculous advice.

SORPRESAS TE DA LA VIDA

I didn't cry when they cut me open.
I didn't cry when Mami told me she was proud.
I didn't cry when I woke up in pain.

When Lala walks in, suddenly I am
a rainstorm. She sits next to my hospital bed
& picks up the phone on the nightstand.

Can we call the chatline on this?
I laugh so hard I almost pop a stitch.
Lala brought Hope a gift.

A tiny onesie with the Puerto Rican flag in the front.
For her first parade, she says.

We gotta make sure she's representing.

HOW WE GOT OUR NAMES
POSTPARTUM DEPRESSION

Dear Hope,

Let's end this story where faith meets Hope.
Isn't it weird how a womb is the only place on the body

that can be both a home and a graveyard?
The sadness tells me I am worth nothing now

that I am a ghost town, a cemetery.
The doctor says my hormones are to blame.

Estrella jokes that at least my hormones
didn't try to kill my baby.

I worry that you will leave me
or worse I will leave you.

Until then, I promise—
No, I'll have faith

that I'll always give you
the most habitable parts of me.

The parts that made it.

VISITING DANNY

This is your tío Danny.
I help Danny hold his niece.

This is where he lives.
Brooklyn is our island.

& I promise that Hope
will know her history.

WHAT IF MAKING IT LOOKS LIKE THIS

What if making it happens every day.

To each of us. Differently.

Hear me out.
I'm saying:

What if making it is trying to find good news
on a bad news day.

Or the corner boys finding safety
on the street that everybody fears.

What if making it is finally affording a pizza dinner
or a really good acrylic nail set.

Or having just enough money to buy maxi pads.
What if making it takes the train

from The Bronx to Brooklyn every day.
What if making it plays dominoes on the corner

of Starr Street and Knickerbocker
and doesn't get kicked out by the cops.

What if making it peddles a broken shopping cart
with enough groceries for three days

and dances in the line at the food pantry.
What if it sells maví.

What if making it is saying today is wack
& it hopes tomorrow is better.

What if making it is not answering the teacher
when she says your name wrong.

What if making it takes naps or laughs loud in class.
What if it creates poems that no one will ever see.

What if making it is Diasporican.
What if it is still learning how it got here.

What if making it drops out of school.
What if making it gives birth to hope.

What if making it learns every day it is alive
is a part of history.

What if making it is today, is yesterday,
is tomorrow.

What if it is the very basic act of breathing.

ACKNOWLEDGMENTS

Wow. We made it. Thank you.

If I have forgotten your name in these pages please forgive me or send me a text or email so that I can tell you how sorry I am and how much I appreciate you.

Let's start with my children. Lisa, thank you for choosing me to be your mother over and over again. I am so proud of who you already are and who you are becoming. To the stars, my love. Adrian, your wisdom astonishes me, your laugh replenishes me, your questions help me grow. I love you both more than I have the vocabulary to express.

To my super dope, super fly editor, Nancy Mercado, thank you for taking a chance on an Instagram poet from Bushwick. I am forever grateful. Forever ever. Immense gratitude to Dial Books and the entire team at Penguin Books, Lauri Hornik, Rosie Ahmed, Regina Castillo, Margarita Javier, Kenny Young, Jason Henry, Theresa Evangelista, Vanessa DeJesús, and all of the folks behind the scenes who helped bring my dream into the physical realm.

To Fanesha Fabre, girlllllll. Thank you for saying yes to being my cover artist. I am forever in awe of your skill, passion, and vision. Pa' lante.

Katherine Latshaw, I am so grateful for your representation, your belief in this book, and your incredibly impressive email response rate to my thousand questions.

Okay, y'all know this book would not be possible without poets. Vamo a empezar por ahi.

To Rich Villar, thank you for saying yes when I asked for mentorship many moons ago. To Caridad La Bruja De La Luz, your light beamed in such a way that it reached the young girl in Brooklyn who was living in the dark. To Miguel Algarín, the house you built gave birth to me, thank you. To Mahogany L. Browne, Jive Poetic, and the entire Nuyorican Poets Cafe family, you showed me that it was possible to dream out loud. To Elizabeth Acevedo, thank you for paving paths & guiding first-time authors down them. To Ocean Vuong, thank you for the time you took to talk poems with me one summer afternoon at Poets House. Vanessa Hidary, thank you for always championing me, celebration at Bodega soon! Nicholasa Mohr, for your dedication to the stories of Nuyorican femmes. Willie Perdomo, for being the realest, I picked up a pen immediately after hearing you spit for the first time. Sandra Cisneros, you are the reason so many of us found our home in literature.

This work would not be possible without my literary ancestors, Tato Laviera, Pedro Pietri, Judith Ortiz Cofer, Luisa Capetillo, Jesús Colón, Pura Belpré, Juan Antonio Corretjer, and so many more Boricua literary pioneers. Thank you for your work in the world. I hope my work does you justice.

To all of the homies & original Bushwick heads still doing work in or about the community long before and after it was forgotten. I see you. We out here. Flako Jimenez, Vanessa Mártir, Danielle De Jesus— they said we wouldn't make it. They lied. I'm so proud of us. Seguimos!

Gratitude to *Latina* magazine, who published "To All the Black & Brown Girls Who Go Missing Before They Go Missing," an earlier version of "Estrella Goes Missing" and to *Muzzle* magazine, who published "Psych Ward," an earlier version of the poem "Psychological Evaluation."

I'd like to thank the church basement in Bedstuy, Brooklyn, for hosting the program that helped me earn my GED as well as all of the adult educators who believe that high school drop-outs deserve to make it too. On that same note, shout-out to everyone in educational justice work. Special shout-out to Integrate NYC, Coalition for Educational Justice, Teens Take Charge, Educolor, New Yorkers for Racially Just Public Schools, and everyone who believes and works towards equitable education.

Thank you to the homies, Zarah Peña, Joel Sahadath, Annette Estevez, Jasmine Aequitas, Michelle Cardona, Alberto Bruno, Stephanie Velazquez, Vanessa Castro, Angelique Imani Rodriguez, Keomi Tarver, Wendy Vaquer, Jasmine Rodriguez, Cheila Reyes, for helping shape parts of who I grew into, for lifting me in my lowest moments, coming to my shows, listening to me talk about this book and for loving me so wholly.

Thank you to the following teachers who guided my early works and my understanding of craft. Chris Abani, r. erica doyle, John Murillo, Phillip Metres.

Honorable mentions and special shout-outs to Salsa music, my beta readers, The Bible, my social media cousins, P.S. 123, Enrico Fermi Intermediate School, indie booksellers everywhere, bookstagrammers, Bushwick Public Library, affordable housing, the MTA, everybody navigating the NYC welfare system, and anyone who had to survive Bushwick when it was unsurvivable.

Thank you to my immediate family.

Mami, Papi, Marilyn, Keko, Jahaira, Ashley, Ralph, Luis.

Jon, thank you for showing me that love is a series of actions.

To the people who have fought and continuously fight for the independence & liberation of Puerto Rico. I understand myself better because of you. Hasta la libertad!

I honor my abuelas who have passed on and continually guide me: Gabriela Hernandez, Carmen Rosa Velasquez.

RESOURCES

There aren't too many safe adults in Sarai's story. I hope you have safe adults in your life who actively listen to you without judgement and who see and believe you when you tell them what you are experiencing. Here are some resources in case you don't know any safe adults.

Crisis Text Line
Available 24/7
Support to all individuals
in crisis
Text "HELLO" to 741741
www.crisistextline.org

SAMSHA
Substance Abuse & Mental
Health Services Administration

Available 24/7
1-800-662-HELP (4357)
https://www.samhsa.gov/

The Trevor Project
Available 24/7
Confidential suicide hotline
for LGBT youth
866-488-7386
https://www.thetrevorproject.org/

Therapy For Black Girls
Online resource directory of therapists dedicated to encouraging the mental wellness of Black women and girls.
https://therapyforblackgirls.com/

Therapy For Latinx
Online resource directory of therapists dedicated to encouraging the mental wellness of Latinx people.
https://www.therapyforlatinx.com/

National Domestic Violence
Available 24/7
Supports individuals who are experiencing domestic violence
Hotline 1-800-799-7233 (SAFE)
http://www.thehotline.org/

National Suicide Hotline
Available 24/7
1-800-273-8255
https://suicidepreventionlifeline.org

Child HELP USA National
Hotline
Available 24/7
1-800-4-A-CHILD
(1-800-422-4453)
http://www.childhelpusa.org/

National Teen Dating Violence Hotline
Available 24/7
Questions or concerns about dating relationships
1-866-331-9474

Text "loveis" 22522
http://www.loveisrespect.org

The Anti-Violence Project
Available 24/7, English and Spanish, LGBT-inclusive
Support for individuals who have suffered violence
Hotline 212-714-1124
http://www.avp.org

National Sexual Assault Hotline
Available 24/7
Supports victims of sexual assault, LGBT-inclusive
1-800-656-HOPE 24/7 or Online Counseling at www.rainn.org

National Runaway Switchboard
Available 24/7
Confidential hotline supports runaway youth for safety
800-RUNAWAY (786-2929)
www.1800RUNAWAY.org

Trans Lifeline
Available 24/7
Hotline staffed by volunteers who are all trans-identified and educated in the range of difficulties transgender people experience
U.S. (877) 565-8860
Canada (877) 330-6366
http://www.translifeline.org

POEMS IN CONVERSATION

The poem "Can I Be Puerto Rican?" is in conversation with:
Nuyorican Poet Mariposa's "Ode to the Diasporican"

The poem "Fiao" is in conversation with
Nuyorican Poet Pedro Pietri's "Puerto Rican Obituary"

The poem "The War on Roaches" is in conversation with
Lucille Clifton's "Cruelty"

The poem "How We Got Our Names: Raid" is
in conversation with Pedro Pietri's "Suicide Note From
a Cockroach in a Low Income Project"

The poem "If Being Boricua in Bushwick is a Feeling—
It's the Best Kind" is in conversation with
Jacqueline Woodson's "Bushwick History Lesson"

The poem "Ask Me Anything Day with Ms. Rivera" is in
conversation with Sandra Cisneros's "Those Who Don't"

The poem "The Daily News Says" is in conversation with
Nikki Giovanni's "Nikki-Rosa"

The poem "Things We Don't Talk About: Color" is
in conversation with Fortunato Vizcarrondo's
"¿Y tu agüela, aonde ejtá?"

The poem "The Apartment on Troutman Street" is an
homage to Sandra Cisneros's "The House on Mango Street"

The poem "Your Silence Will Not Protect You" is an homage to
Audre Lorde's essay, *The Transformation of Silence into
Language and Action.*